The Boy

NAEEM MURR

The Boy

HOUGHTON MIFFLIN COMPANY
BOSTON · NEW YORK
1998

For information about permission to reproduce
selections from this book, write to Permissions,
Houghton Mifflin Company, 215 Park Avenue
South, New York, New York 10003.

*Library of Congress
Cataloging-in-Publication Data*
Murr, Naeem.
The boy / Naeem Murr.
p. cm.
ISBN 0-395-90106-5
I. Title.
PS3563.U7637B69 1998
813'.54 — dc21   97-49150 CIP

Book design by Robert Overholtzer

Printed in the United States of America

QUM 10 9 8 7 6 5 4 3 2 1

FOR THE TWO OF YOU

I WOULD LIKE TO
GRATEFULLY ACKNOWLEDGE

———————

Dawn Seferian, Katie Owen,
Louise Quayle, Bill Hamilton,
Chris Wiman, Pimone Triplett,
and Peter Stitt.

The Boy

1

IN A WAY it is a perfect place for a body. A body, not a corpse — corpse is too ghoulish, too final. On the south side of the Thames, you walk down from Hammersmith Bridge toward Mortlake along the towpath. After about half a mile you see it, a derelict brewery, a vast Victorian red-brick, rows of windows all boarded up except for those at the very top — in which every lead-framed pane has been broken by the ambitious stones of children. Go around the back of the building, out of sight of the towpath and the river. The boards have been pulled away from one of the windows, the window itself smashed in. Enter now. It's damp, as you would expect; water, brought high by some capillary action, streams in places down the walls. You make your way past vast, rusting vats, and into a room on the river side of the brewery. Here the ceiling rises sixty feet above you, and upon it swarms sunlight reflected up from the river. Massive square columns thrust down from that light, whittling into the darkness where you stand. But it's not complete darkness; there's a faint precipitate of light, and it's by this, as you move across the concrete floor toward a kind of alcove, fragments of glass crunching beneath your feet, that you see the body — or think you do — part of it, anyway; the legs perhaps, the bare legs, legs like sleep.

He wasn't soulless. Some might claim it, but I think few would believe it. And as for what the boy believed, well, this gravid, this damp silence, this lime dust (I think of lime upon his lips), this vermicular play of light, this echo of water, perhaps they speak for him.

I shall tell you what I know. The names I shall use are not, of course, the real names, though they have a personal resonance for me. But otherwise, from what I tell you, I've removed myself as neatly as a skin blemish is removed by a laser. And like a blemish I was, at once, part of and superfluous to the body of this story, easy to remove, though you may notice the vaguest scar.

2

SEAN HENNESSY HAD ARRIVED. He stood for a moment at the wrought-iron gate of the Churchill Home for Boys — an enormous, decrepit Georgian house in Battersea. He tried to think again — or rather, not to think — of what he would do if the boy was here. Would the boy run? Would he realize that Sean knew what he'd done? Still he did not enter the gate, was not merely equivocating, but was at the threshold of something as untenable to his mind as the night is to a single light — a light about which all his civilized feelings hazed like insects.

He was a tall, slender man, his dark hair thick and a little unkempt. His sharp, generously proportioned nose gave a prowlike thrust to his face; and yet, about his eyes there was something not flinching exactly — their coarse brows making them even slightly belligerent — but reticent and insular.

Finally he entered the gate, made his way to the door, and rang the bell. On the far side of the gravel courtyard, to the right of the house, two boys of about fifteen were taking apart the engine of an old Cortina. The sight of one of them in particular, a slender boy who'd brightly hennaed his hair, panicked Sean again. What would he do if the boy was here? Christ, the boy might even embrace him. For so long after he'd found the diary, he'd felt just rage, a rage that would turn everything ashen.

He rang again, waited a few more minutes, and as he was about to ring for the third time the door was opened by a diminutive, painfully gaunt woman of about forty-five. Her soft, shapeless shoes and the oversized silver crucifix that hung about her neck made Sean think of a nun.

"Have you been ringing for long?" she asked with a kind of irritated solicitousness as she drew a pair of thick gardening gloves from her hands. "I was in the back."

"No, not long." He cleared his throat. "My name's Sean Hennessy. I'm looking for a boy. He — "

Suddenly noticing the boys at the car, she cut him off, shouting, "You saw him here. Why didn't you tell him to go round the back? Get your heads on. And Kyle, didn't I tell you to take the rubbish out this morning?" She addressed Sean again, rapid and irritated: "If you're looking for a boy, you can have either of those for nothing."

"Is Mr. Reardon in?" Sean asked.

Her eyes, at once insomniac and penetrating, flickered over his face.

"Ronan's upstairs with his mother," she replied coldly, obviously resenting his appeal to another authority. "He won't be down until six. I'm his wife, Theresa. So who are you looking for?"

He found it strange that she hadn't asked him in. Indeed, she'd even edged forward a little in the doorway as if to pressure him back.

"Well, let me tell you my situation," Sean said. "I once fostered a boy who, I understand, after — " he faltered, her gaze unsettling him, "after the period of foster care terminated, came here. We called him — he liked us to call him — Pierce, but I believe his original name was Tobias, Tobias Forrester; and he also went by the name of Durward."

At this, she pressed her thin lips together, and all that remained of her responsiveness to him vanished.

The awkward silence lengthened, but finally she said, with a smile that looked utterly stranded upon her still reluctant mouth, "Three aliases and barely into his teens. Sounds like a criminal."

It wasn't a no, so Sean waited.

"We've had a lot of boys here," she said after a moment. "They come and they move on. Get fostered. Run away. I don't remember a Pierce or a Tobias at any time. Or a Durward."

"I do know he came here," Sean said, taking the boy's photograph out of his pocket. She looked down at it, but her eyes were blank, receiving nothing. "Obviously he's a few years older now," Sean prompted, barely disguising his irritation at her deliberate obtuseness.

Just then the front gate squealed open. Looking back, Sean saw, hurrying up to the door, a tall, pretty young woman with an alert and engagingly impudent face. When she arrived, breathless, she surveyed Sean candidly for a moment with her bright, slightly bulbous eyes, and then stooped in a kind of mock supplication to Theresa.

"Oh my God, you would *not* believe what's just happened to me," she cried out, at once appalled and amused, as she cast another glance at Sean. "A man had some kind of seizure on the bus. I kept thinking, Oh my God I'm going to have to give him the kiss of life. I mean no disrespect to the man, but he had a mouth like a bulldog's backside. I just bought myself a pair of nylons, and I kept thinking, if I have to give him the kiss of life, I don't care what anyone says, I'm going to do it *through* the nylons." She pulled up suddenly, her eyes falling on the photograph.

"No!" she cried out incredulously. "That's not Devon, is it? Would you look at that, Theresa, it's Devon."

"Devon?" Sean said, looking to Theresa for confirmation; but she refused to face him, her hollow cheeks now speckled red.

The young woman took hold of the photograph. "You see I was right about him dyeing his hair," she said to Theresa, adding to Sean: "He's gone blond." She pondered the photograph for a moment longer, musing finally, "Isn't he just the most beautiful boy in the world? Too beautiful even to dream about." She laughed, giving Sean a roguish look, "Not, of course, that I dream about any of the boys here."

Theresa remained silent, staring into the ground, absently toying with her crucifix, and the young woman suddenly became aware that something was wrong.

"It's definitely Devon, isn't it? — isn't it, Theresa?" she asked, now a little more tentative.

6

"I suppose it could be," Theresa replied flatly, without looking up.

The young woman again examined the photograph, obviously checking if her assessment was beyond all reasonable doubt. Sean, his heart beating hard, kept his eyes upon her.

She obviously decided it was, and with the flicker of an impatient frown said pointedly to Theresa, "Well, I'm surprised *you* didn't recognize him."

"Is this boy here?" Sean cut in, trying to hide his agitation.

"Oh no, he's gone," the young woman replied blithely, turning those brimming eyes to him. "He disappeared a few months after I started here."

"Which was when?" Sean asked.

"Almost five months ago now." Looking down at the photograph again, she became a little abstracted. "I remember he was just so charming. Those *incredible* eyes of his. One time he — "

Touching her wrist gently with his hand, Sean interrupted with a soft, exasperated imperativeness: "Do you know where he's gone?"

"No," she said, a little more seriously, "but he was quite close to Ronan" — she glanced at Theresa — "And you too, Theresa . . . I thought."

"If we're talking about Devon," Theresa slowly replied, measuring out words that she seemed to have been preparing in her silence, "I was close to him in as much as I was helping him with some spiritual matters." She looked up at Sean, her face hard, accusatory. "He was a deeply spiritual child, but he'd been let down so many times by those who . . ." But her words evaporated in the angry resolution with which Sean confronted her stare, and she quickly truckled.

After a moment, Sean said, "I'd really like to talk to Mr. Reardon. I'll come back at six."

The young woman checked her watch. "Well, it's ten to five now. Why don't you come in and have a cup of tea?"

Theresa looked for a moment as if she were about to protest this, but then turned around and walked quickly back through the house and into the garden.

After a brief, quizzical frown that conveyed to Sean her perplexity at Theresa's behavior, the young woman said, "I'm Caitlín," and offered her hand.

He followed her into the hallway. The house, though bright and homely in its furnishings, had the generic air of an institution, and as he entered, Sean imagined the boy entering for the first time: the vase of carnations on the sideboard, the foggy, full-length mirror, the framed picture of a seahorse, and that smell, that datum of ammonia, mnemonically brutal — *brutal*. It said you'd arrived nowhere. Again. For a second Sean felt in his stomach that sensation one gets when one descends in a lift too quickly.

"Peace," Caitlín called back as he followed her into the bright, open-plan dining room, sitting room, and kitchen. "At least until six or so. Most of the boys are off on a trip to see the HMS *Belfast*."

She was nervous now, he could tell. This was exactly how Rea had been, by turns bold, funny, intimate, even with strangers, and then behaving as if she didn't trust herself to make a cup of tea competently. And like his ex-wife, this woman had the most beautiful hair, almost down to her waist, though hers was a dark brown, while his wife's had been blonde — was blonde. Like Rea, this woman used her hair to create a kind of sweetly coy context for her brashness, pulling it over one shoulder and cushioning her cheek into it. But unlike his wife, she was very tall, her body remarkably slender, without breasts or hips. Even through her lazy, careful grace he could see all that awkwardness of her adolescence, that time in her life when she'd stood a good few inches above even the tallest boys, her body not developed, just long, ungainly, splaying out from her small school desk; so she grew her hair, pulled her legs together, contained and concealed herself in one supple curve. And just now, at thirty, thirty-five? she was growing into herself. Sean remembered, when he'd loved his wife most intensely, how he'd wished to possess each moment of her, each incarnation — as a child, as an adolescent, as a woman — possess her knowing what she would become: not this brattish child, not this painfully shy adolescent, but that woman who was, to each man she left or who left her, his one deep regret, a fog in his limbs. Indeed, perhaps it was this desire to possess her so completely that had made him wish to have a daughter, had made the happiest day of his life the day when Megan was born.

Trembling now, Sean felt a faint nausea of grief, a heaviness to his breath, as if a black and viscous liquid had pooled in his lungs.

Caitlín brought him a mug of tea and emptied a pack of chocolate digestives onto a plate in front of him, all of this not done *by* but *from* her long, covert body.

"You'll have to forgive me," she said, going back to the kitchen area. "I have to make dinner for the mob."

Still recovering, Sean nodded vaguely.

"So why are you looking for Devon?" she called a moment later, dicing onions.

"I fostered him for a while," Sean said, "for almost five years, in fact. Unfortunately things ended rather badly for us, and there's something now I need to talk to him about." He avoided her eyes as he said this, those round eyes, at once candid and canny, which seemed hardly to blink. He was very bad even at half-concealing the truth.

"Did you get at all close to him?" he asked, finally looking up.

She couldn't answer for a moment because she'd put a whole vanilla cream into her mouth from a packet she'd just opened. A little embarrassed, she covered her lips with her hand, then said, as she quickly chewed, swallowed, and cleaned her teeth with her tongue, "Don't you think there's something about women and sugar? I'm going to eat this whole packet of biscuits. It's a special gift I have." And with that she slipped another biscuit under her hand and into her mouth.

He smiled. "You remind me of someone," he said.

"Please don't say your ex-wife," Caitlín called, sweeping the onions into an enormous pot. "Someone said that to me in the Hare and Hounds last night."

He laughed.

"It *is* your ex-wife," she cried with mock injury.

"But my ex-wife was . . . wonderful."

"So where is she now?" Theresa asked, pulling half a dozen packets of minced beef out of the fridge.

"I don't know," Sean replied quietly.

Caitlín blushed as she opened the packets.

After a moment, she said, "He was a great favorite with Theresa. And the boys loved him, most of them — even the alpha males. They might know where he is. Daniel, especially. Daniel adored him. All of them adored him really. Devon had quite a little entourage. Which is funny, because when I remember him, I remember him being alone — which I know is not accurate." She froze pensively for a moment as she was crumbling the meat into the pot, and as if to clarify it as much to herself as to him, added, "Perhaps because that seemed his *condition,* if you know what I mean. Being alone."

"I do," Sean said, feeling the boy's presence as something palpable in this woman's consciousness, feeling even envious of the absorbed remembering that momentarily emptied her face.

Now she made a surreptitious glance toward the doorway into the hall, and said, sotto voce, "I don't know what Ronan thought of him really. He always praised him to the skies, but Ronan likes the boys to focus their affections on him. Not in any bad way, but he's . . . you know." She blushed a little at her own indiscretion; then, making a joke of it, said, "Like the rest of us he just wants to be loved. . . .

Anyway," she added more seriously, "he always seemed a little unsettled when Devon was about. He also let him break the rules, which I found very strange."

"What did you think of him?" Sean said.

"Devon? Oh, he terrified me. He has this capacity — you must have experienced it yourself — to become invisible. So often I'd be doing something — making dinner, cleaning up, whatever — thinking I was alone, often talking to myself like an idiot, having imaginary arguments — *Les Mots d'Escalier,* that would be the title of my autobiography — and then suddenly I'd see him, sitting in one of those armchairs, or standing in the doorway, watching me, as if he'd been watching me for hours. And I just couldn't look into his face, that beautiful, *beautiful* face of his. He made me feel as if I were thirteen again. Even just the night after I first met him — " Suddenly she pulled up, paused, took a breath.

"You know," she said, her tone returning to earth, "this is my problem. My brother used to hate it. He said I had absolutely no sense of discretion or of when intimacy was appropriate. I remember one time he brought a friend of his home, and at the dinner table I said something about hoping my breasts would grow before I got to university. My brother just exploded — right in front of the poor guy . . . ugh!" In this last despairing grunt, Sean could see how instantaneously available, how quick her whole emotional life was in her. "But intimacy," she went on, "is only intimacy, surely, if it's instinctive — that's what I used to tell my husband."

Sean didn't know how to respond.

"You see, I've done it again."

"Well, what were you going to say . . . about the boy?"

"Nothing, nothing," she said, seeming annoyed, frustrated at her own incontinence. "I'll tell you some other time."

Sean didn't insist, though he was desperate to know. After a moment, he said, "Do you know of anywhere I can stay around here?"

She looked surprised: "Where have you come from?"

"Birmingham. That's where I live."

"And you're going to stay?"

"I have to find him."

"Well how long are you planning to stay?"

"*Until* I find him."

She gave him a more serious look.

"I *need* to find out something from him," Sean said in answer to it.

She stirred the sauce for a moment. Finally she said, "Well, I live on a boat about ten minutes away from here, and I know there's a couple of free rooms on that. I mean they're basically rabbit hutches, but it's only thirty pounds a week."

Sean nodded. "Thank you. That sounds fine."

She put on a huge pot of water to boil and came to sit down with Sean. As absent and out of sync as she made herself out to be, she sat with consummate elegance, her long legs together, her long hair pulled over one side of her face. It was catlike, at once supple and constrained. He noticed she'd finished the packet of biscuits she'd opened in the kitchen, and now began to make disappear with an expert sleight of hand the ones she'd poured onto the plate in front of him.

"So you've been working here just for a few months?" Sean asked.

"I'm on placement," she said. "I want to be a social worker. I know it's a bit late in life to begin a career."

"What were you doing before?"

"Oh, being a wife to the sweetest man on earth. And then I discovered that though I didn't mind looking at his face straight on, I just couldn't stand his profile." She turned to Sean with a slightly perplexed expression. "Does that seem strange to you?"

"Not in the context of you," Sean said, smiling.

This smile seemed to touch something off in her. Her eyes widened with that naive, amazed look of hers, and playfully she constrained her own roguish smile.

"He thinks I'm adorably clumsy, that I dropped him inadvertently, like I used to drop everything of value in our house. He liked it. He used to buy expensive things because he knew that eventually I would knock them onto the floor. And then he could forgive me. Sweet really."

"So is he still waiting for you to pick him up and put him together?"

"I think he is."

"Is that a possibility?"

"No. This is the kind of consciousness that should have come to me when I was twenty, but I'm thirty. With him, as with any man when I was that age, I was just so amazed and so grateful that he liked me."

"Why would *you* be amazed?" His emphasis was too obviously a compliment. She released her smile a little and he felt himself blush.

"I don't know. I always am amazed. It's not that I lack confidence, but it still amazes me when men want to think of me as anything more than a friend. And with him my amazement lasted seven years. Then one evening — I remember it so well — we were both in the sitting room. I was trying to read, but there was this noise that was annoying me — infuriating me. I couldn't locate it at first, and then I realized that it was the sound of him swallowing his tea. And I looked over at him, his profile, he was reading the paper. . . . And that was it."

Now she looked directly into Sean's eyes. "What happened with your wife?"

He frowned, rubbed his warm cheek for a moment. "Ah . . . well . . ." he stammered.

There came the sound of footsteps down the stairs, light and rapid. A small man with a bald head and rather hircine features stormed in. Sean stood up to introduce himself as the man came to an irresolute halt. His eyes, deep-set beneath beetle brows, flickered from Caitlín to Sean as he tugged compulsively at the immaculate silver goatee that surrounded his sharp little mouth. But he seemed too consumed with fury to assimilate them.

"Mr. Reardon?" Sean began, offering his hand.

But the man cut him off. "If there is a God," he shouted, "then *God* love her."

"Theresa's out in the garden," Caitlín said quickly.

The man stormed out of the back door.

A second later they heard again from the garden: "If there is a God, then *God* love her . . . and God *give me strength.*"

Through the doorway, Sean watched Theresa, who'd been pollarding some rose bushes, approach her husband.

"It's his mother," Caitlín whispered. "She drives him insane, just tortures him. She's a chronic diabetic, won't go into a home and won't take her insulin. He called me one time in a panic when he'd been delayed at the police station because one of the boys had been caught shoplifting. I ran up there but she'd already slipped into some kind of coma so I just called the ambulance."

Sean looked again out of the back door. Theresa seemed to have calmed Ronan down completely, was holding both his hands as if to constrain him, and whispering earnestly. Whatever she was saying caused Ronan to glance back through the doorway at Sean, who felt suddenly voyeuristic and sat down again.

A few moments later, Ronan reentered the house. Nothing of his former fury remained. He approached Sean wearing a smile so unctuous it seemed about to slide right off his face, and offered his hand. Like a politician or a priest, he took Sean's hand in both of his, and didn't release it. Though it was a gentle, even warm hold, it put Ronan completely in control.

"I understand you're looking for one of our boys," he said in a voice incongruously deep and resonant for such a fastidious little man.

Sean introduced himself and then extricated his hand from Ronan's persistent grasp in order to show him the photo.

"It's a boy I fostered some years ago. Apparently he called himself Devon while he was here."

Like his wife, Ronan stared at the photograph without really looking at it.

"Well, it may be," he said, "but Devon's gone. He ran away. We informed the police, of course, but the truth is that he was never really happy here — he was rather advanced for his age. Is it rude of me to ask you exactly why you're looking for him?"

"I'm looking for him because I feel he may have taken something I said rather badly."

Ronan laughed, a humorless laugh, the laugh of someone who has long put aside any real or innocent pleasure in life. "You've left it rather late."

"I have," Sean said simply, "but it's important to me."

Ronan regarded him steadily, seriously for a few moments.

"Well, I don't think you're going to have much luck. From what little I remember of him, I do remember that he often expressed his hatred of London. My suspicion is that he went to Cornwall, which he'd formulated, if memory serves, as a kind of heaven on earth. Lots of happy memories there apparently — or perhaps just the few happy memories he had. You see, he'd been treated badly and let down by so many people. . . ." This last comment carried a reproach, and there was a vague vindictiveness in

Ronan's face, as if he were stabbing a needle into a small effigy of Sean.

Theresa now stood at the back door, her large gardening gloves still on, her arms crossed. She was an adamant figure, something sharp caught in the throat of the room, choking everything. She wanted him gone, Sean could tell, and this man too, with his fake smile, wanted him gone.

"I wonder if I could talk to some of the boys?" Sean said.

"I don't see the point of that," Ronan quickly replied, his smile suddenly withering, his tone impatient. "The boys stick together. They'll either say nothing or lie to you."

"I would still like to try," Sean said.

"Well . . ." Ronan drew out with a negative intonation; but just at that moment the house flooded with shouts and the sound of feet thudding up the stairs.

The boys were back.

3

DINNER was a pleasantly anarchic affair, a mound of spaghetti, a vat of sauce, and a steaming bowl of cauliflower that Caitlín had skillfully boiled to the very point before complete dissolution. Throughout the preparations, Sean had watched, had taken in, her odd, sweet, incompetent efficiency.

Looking around the table at faces flecked with spaghetti sauce, hanging low over their plates, he imagined the boy here, and at the sight of some of the younger boys thought also of his own real son, Liam.

"Who are you?" one of the boys finally asked, a plump, cheeky child of about twelve, whose red hair seemed already to be receding.

"My name's Sean. I'm here because I'm looking for a boy called Devon."

At this the boy who'd spoken glanced nervously at a couple of the other boys. The silence suddenly lost its appetite, became tense, airless.

"Daniel," Caitlín called from the kitchen, where she was

cutting slices of ginger cake, "you were close to Devon. This man was his foster father. It's important he finds him."

Daniel, who was perhaps fourteen or fifteen but small for his age, his blunt, freckled face lined with worry, blushed and looked cornered.

"I'm not the police or anything," Sean assured him. "As Caitlín said, I was his foster father for a while and I'd like to get in touch with him, see how he's doing. I have some things of his that he might want."

But Daniel just stared down at his plate and toyed with the remains of his food — as did all the rest at the table except one, a lanky boy with terrible acne. Wearing a smile that was at once craven and contemptuous, this boy surveyed the bowed heads of the others. Sean could see immediately that this child extracted some necessary, bitter pleasure from being outcast, hated.

Finally this boy settled his eyes upon Sean and said, "'E's rentin' i'n' 'e — "

"Shu' up!" shouted Daniel. Another boy, a skinhead, banged the heel of his fork against the table.

"What's going on?" Caitlín called from the kitchen.

"It's all right," Sean reassured her, adding quickly to the acned boy, "Renting? Renting what?"

A small outbreak of laughter was extinguished quickly by the uncompromising gazes of Daniel and the skinhead. The acned boy didn't say another word, though he smiled to himself with grim satisfaction.

After dinner, Caitlín called her landlord and arranged for Sean to take one of the cabins on a week-to-week basis.

Sean had wanted to speak to Ben, the boy with the acned face, but as soon as the meal had finished, the boy had run out of the house.

"Ben won't be back until late," Caitlín said with a squeamish look. "I think Daniel and Steve have it in for him."

Sean sighed, trying to rub the frown from his forehead. Just a few hours ago it had all seemed within his grasp, and now the boy was as far away from him as ever.

Caitlín convinced Sean that there was no point in him staying any longer and promised that she would try to get hold of Ben before the other boys did to ask him if he knew anything else. She gave him directions to the boat and told him that the landlord would meet him on the wharf at eight.

Sean left. It was completely dark and had just started to drizzle. Daniel and the skinhead were hanging around at the front gate of the home waiting, he knew, for Ben.

He took a right onto Lexington Street, which, Caitlín had told him, would lead him directly to the towpath, and as he passed a derelict church, a shadow split from the dark mouth of its arched entrance and cut quickly over to him. It was Ben, grinning as if in defiant anticipation of the blows that would surely rain down on him later.

"Eh up, chief," he said with slack insouciance, trying to produce an arrogant swagger from his thin body, his hands jammed into his pockets.

"Do you know where he is?" Sean said directly.

"You got any fags?" Ben said, holding up two fingers, his hand trembling.

Sean shook his head.

"Will you get me some from the Paki shop then?" Ben gave Sean a speculative look that was, by turns, flinching and insolent. He was obviously trying to assess how much his information was worth.

Sean realized that he was being asked to play a part, so after pausing for just long enough to give Ben's speculation something to live upon, he nodded and let Ben lead him through a few streets to a small newsagents.

Outside, Ben made his demands: "I want fo'r'y B 'n' H and I want a dirty mag — 'ustler — and I want a pound of bonbons, the yella ones." He spoke in a brittle, imperative tone, which he no doubt hoped would sound masterful, but which resounded with impotence.

When Sean had bought and handed over all he'd asked for, Ben still didn't speak, but began walking back toward Lexington Street, indicating with a jerk of his head for Sean to follow. He was clearly enjoying this unwonted power, his role, and desired to draw it out for as long as possible. Pity as much as prudence kept Sean playing along.

"So why you looking for 'im then?"

"That's my business," Sean said, adopting a gruff terseness that he calculated would fit best into Ben's fantasy. He wondered even if he might have to play a little rough — a prospect he dreaded.

But, prizing the sticky bonbons from his yellowed teeth, Ben finally said, "'E's rentin' in Victoria. Seen 'im up there last Sunday outside the Railway Tavern. You know what I mean by rentin'?"

"Yes," Sean said, "of course. I was just surprised. So do you know where he lives?"

"One my mates says 'e 'as a regular puts 'im up."

"Do you know who? Where?"

Ben shook his head. That was it. That was as much as he knew.

"Thanks," Sean said, forgetting his role and betraying a little tenderness as Caitlín's boat came into sight.

Ben stopped walking. Sean stopped also.

"They're waiting for you," Sean said. "Daniel and that other boy."

Just for a second, Ben looked stricken, a child again, his lips stained with yellow sherbet. But then that brittle defiance, that sly, bitter smile returned.

"I'll be all right. I'll give 'em a butch at my mag," he said, patting the rolled up *Hustler* protruding from his coat pocket and winking as if it were his trump card.

4

UPON HER LIPS Theresa felt the faint pressure of hope and woke. The curtains fluttered inward from the window, which she left open every night in case the boy returned, and his form, his face echoed faintly to another waking, to nothing, the nothing of her sister.

Every night she would wake convinced he was in her room. But nothing; and now it had been almost four months. His absence was like a sickness. She felt for him with an intensity she'd experienced only once before — with that Gothic Jesus she'd seen as a girl when she and her father had been driving to Rome.

A few weeks before her sixteenth birthday, her father, who hadn't been feeling well for a long time, had finally gone to see a doctor because there were spots of blood in his spit. And it was on the very morning of that birthday that he returned from his second appointment to tell her that he'd been diagnosed with a cancer that had begun in his lungs and had now spread to his liver and his spine. He then went up to his room and began to pray.

For five days he ate nothing, drank only water, and prayed, sometimes exhorting God with such impassioned vehemence that Theresa could hear him from downstairs. During those days she too didn't eat, felt hardly able to breathe, existing mutely within his will, while he attempted to talk his way into the will of God. And after the fifth day, he descended the stairs and told her to pack because God had directed him to go to Rome.

To Theresa this seemed inconceivable. Her father had never even left Northern Ireland. He was an intensely private man; when he was not at his actuary office he spent every moment at home. He had no friends, would not suffer visitors, and complained if Theresa ever went out. They didn't even attend church. Instead, for an hour every evening he would read passages to her from the Gospels, and would talk to her about the suffering of Christ in such vivid terms and with such emotion, often crying, that she wondered how these words were different from the Catholic idols he'd warned her against. These devotional sessions would take place in her father's bedroom, a room full of the faint reek of her dead mother, something sweet and rotting that left a residue in her mouth so thick that afterward she would be spitting for hours. They sat opposite each other in excruciating schoolroom chairs, her father, as he paused from his reading, staring up with longing at the plain wooden cross that had belonged to his own father.

Theresa had been terrified of her grandfather, an austere and fervid Protestant, dour and private — a little like her own father except that her grandfather was purely masculine. That was why he'd lived so long. There was no damp in him, the wood of his bones, like the beams of a boat, had been cured in the musty attic of his essential solitude. But his wife, Theresa's grandmother, had worn the red of poppies, the yellow of rapeseed; she was life to the senses, saturated. And she was Catholic — unashamedly so — not in the least afraid or in awe of her ascetic husband.

Theresa's father had become ill, Theresa somehow knew, because within him his mother's blood had caused his father's bones to rot. His mother was corrupting him because he'd tried to bury her within his father — her husband; so Theresa's father's body had become his own mother's unsanctified grave, because he was more his mother's son, but had allowed his father to dominate him, had chosen his father's faith, his austere solitude and masculinity.

So he was going to Rome, to the heart of Catholicism, in an attempt to erase the corruption of time, to regenerate himself by regenerating his mother's body, as the bodies of the Saints, from whose tombs waft sweet odors (like that cloying scent of her mother, more akin to death in life than life in death), are regenerated, their dried, martyred blood after centuries turning liquid. And in going to release his mother perhaps he was going to release his wife also, who'd died just after Theresa was born, and who seemed minutely, myriadly imprisoned in all the photographs of her around the house, staring out of them with an animal confusion, unsmiling; and then to release also his daughter, Theresa's older sister, Catherine, the daughter he'd effaced — they'd both effaced.

Catherine had always refused to succumb to her father's will, to tiptoe around his capricious moods. They fought constantly, because her teachers complained of her missing school, because she smelled of cigarette smoke, because she kept her tampons in full view on the toilet cistern, because she cut a slit up the side of her school skirt. Theresa had loved, hated, and admired her sister so deeply. At night she would sneak into Catherine's room to watch her ritual of preparation: the application of makeup, the trying on and constant checking (in front of the full-length mirror Catherine concealed beneath her mattress) of those outrageous, scanty clothes she hid at the back of her closet. Finally, Catherine would throw on that ridiculously big old leather jacket her boyfriend had given her, lower herself out of the window onto the roof of the shed, into the garden and away.

Sometimes, often on Saturday when her sister had gone shopping, her father downstairs reading the paper or working in his garden, Theresa would take a shower and then slip the leather jacket, which smelled of beer and cigarettes, upon her naked body. Gently, she would run her fingernails over her own skin and press her tightly coupled hands between her legs, so fearful that her father might come in and catch her, for he never allowed them to have locks on their doors, that the image of her father's face, a face at once helpless and haggard with rectitude, became a part of all that she was feeling, that sensuality sealed in the shell of her sister's nights — Oh, God, hadn't they sacrificed each other, hadn't they sacrificed each other? because Catherine was not innocent either: she would tell Theresa (there was a cruelty in this) about all the sinful things she did with her boyfriend in her room when they slipped out of school and returned to the house on Mondays and Thursdays during physics.

Then one Monday morning, Theresa watched Catherine and her boyfriend climb through the broken fence at the back of the school, and after waiting the twenty minutes it would take them to get home telephoned her father at his office to tell him that she'd just had a panic: she'd been ironing her uniform in her sister's room that morning and was sure she'd left the iron on. His office was just ten minutes from their house.

That afternoon when she returned from school, he was lying in his armchair in a strangely matronly pose, his hand wrapped about his forehead, his face blasted into the vacuous amazement of infancy. Over and over again, he was saying, "She's broken my heart. She's dead to me," as if he knew now what these sounds meant, these shibboleths of a sect of ruined men.

Catherine went to stay with a friend from school, then moved to Dublin with her boyfriend. On the day before she left, Catherine waited outside the school for Theresa, cried and said that she would write letters, send them via friends. These letters came, but Theresa never replied, even when they begged, threatened, and finally ended.

At first Theresa was terrified because it seemed that her father would never recover. For weeks after he'd caught them he hardly ate, looked sick, his shell of acetic masculinity shattered as he lay in his chair, staring up into the ceiling like some tragic chatelaine. Then one day a rage seemed to enter him. From all the family albums he removed every picture that contained Catherine and burned them with the compost. But after this, like an invalid who'd snatched at some phantom of energy, he became even more fragile than before. So Theresa took over, tentatively at first, then with an almost euphoric zealotry. Desperate to lift the weight from his shoulders, she removed all trace of her sister from the house — even erased the pencil marks of her sister's heights at different ages from the living room door.

That was just three years before they drove to Rome, to all the missing women — grandmother, mother, daughter — through that sensorium of humming heat that coated her father's face with an impermeable and furious emptiness, his small, blue eyes constantly unsettled. He hadn't known that the liquid in Italy was not, as in Ireland, in the rain and in the grass and in the damp, melancholic souls of its people, but in the languid bodies, the voices, the sheen of sweat, the sunlight upon bronze — nakedness.

In a village near Milan he left Theresa sitting in a plaza for a moment while he went into a bar to ask for directions, and came out to find her smiling down at an Italian boy who was kneeling before her, stroking her cheek with the back of his hand. After this her father hustled her from pensione to pensione, as if she were a prisoner or as if they were eloping.

Some hours before Rome, they stopped outside a small church, which seemed innocent enough, almost derelict, the stucco crumbling. She asked if she could go in to get out of the heat. He hesitated, but perhaps then realized that the next morning they would arrive at the very heart of his mother's idolatrous faith. He told her to go in before him because he wished to pray outside. So entering alone into that damp, cool heat, she saw it at first in silhouette above the altar, and then walked right up to it.

Perhaps she was there just ten minutes before she felt her father's hand hook over the side of her face, taking hold of the bone of her cheek, his fingers pushing into one of her eyes. He hauled her outside and made her kneel down in the singing heat, almost lost in rapeseed, in the yellow blaze of God, which here he could not escape; and he prayed for forgiveness, forcing his hands hard over her eyes, pressing upon the image of the idol until it burst, suffusing a kind of velvet blackness through her limbs, that bloody and almost naked Christ, sinuous, emaciated, white, all the musculature in his legs like woven streams of water, pinioned at his nailed and bloodied feet, liquid pinioned; that raw, soaring Christ, a cloth loose about the cradle of his loins; and when she'd seen him, all her diffuse confusion had found its form. This was Christ, this was the Christ in her father's voice, the Christ he'd wept over, and as if she'd broken some vacuum all her mute guilt flooded into that idol.

That night, when her father's breathing had become rhythmic and deep, like her sister she threw on a heavy coat and slipped out of the pensione (remembered still the beat of her heart and the marble stairway and the man behind the desk at the entrance who looked up at her, said something with a smile as if she were going out to meet her lover). The front door of the church was locked. She tried to lift herself up to one of the windows, but the stucco gave way. Despite falling heavily she felt nothing in her desperation. As she rounded the church, she saw a small door, slightly ajar, from which light emanated. She entered. In a room just off to the right sat a man with his back to her, working on what looked like the inside of a radio. Silently, she passed along the corridor and entered the church. Here and there a few votive candles flickered in the darkness. She took one of the lit candles and knelt down before the Christ, tremulous, feeling as she'd felt when she wore that leather jacket, and more, the nerves in her scalp and down her back like an infestation, unbearably alive, and a strange heaviness in her loins, a heaviness that sent its roots almost painfully up into her stomach. And in this she felt all His pain, and all her love in His limbs, those rootlike limbs, pushing up into her. Shuddering, she'd stifled her cry by pressing her mouth to His bloodied feet.

5

THE FOSTER BOY came today. His name is Pierce and he's
twelve, just a month older than Liam, but he seems much
older, almost my age. I saw him first from the top of the
stairs, and he looked like a girl when he came in — his long
hair and the way the light caught his face in the hallway. It's
so strange. I feel as if Dad got him to replace Liam. Liam's
asthma is so bad now he can hardly walk even to Luxton's
and back. Lots of people in the world. I suppose it doesn't
matter if one comes to replace another. Perhaps this Pierce
has come to replace me. Maybe that's why I thought he
looked like a girl.

Dad often wonders, I'm sure, what he did to make us so
brittle. He thinks too much. Perhaps, for those who think,
reproduction is becoming a lost skill, because they are too
far from their hands, because they leave it too late.

I cut my finger this morning, chopping onions. The cut

didn't bleed at first, as if it were amazed, like men in the
movies when they're killed — powerful, evil men. Their
eyes go wide because they're dead. And that was my finger
with the cut in it. For a second, wide eyes, and then I
pushed at the skin (the hero pulled out his sword) and it
gaped. And then streams of blood. I just couldn't stop looking at it. I wondered what would happen if I kept letting it
bleed. When would I know I was dead? When would it be
too late? Like that time in Spain when I was swimming in
the ocean and I kept thinking, I could just take one more
stroke and then it would be too far for me to get back. And
the ocean would roll me and move me, and I would be in
Dad's head, a little corpse in the dark ocean of his sleep.

Dad has no dreams, he tells me, but I think his sleep is a
dark ocean full of little corpses. He's like the Colossus,
bestride the ocean. He's bronze, and like any statue can fall,
can be taken to pieces, melted down. But the <u>idea</u> of him,
the idea in the word "colossus" and "bestride," cannot be
destroyed. He has a mind of bronze. I said this once to
Mum and she started to cry. I felt bad. She doesn't understand me; she doesn't understand that none of the things I
say are bad things, that there are no bad things.

Mum caught me scraping the blood-soaked onions into
the pan and went berserk. She doesn't like blood. When I
told her last month that I was bleeding between my legs, she
told me what to do to "staunch" it. It makes me feel dirty,
the whole thing. Bandaging my finger, she told me that she
was going to take me to see a doctor who would help me to
stop being so sad all the time. She didn't want to tell Dad.

She said that she'd tried to understand me, that she'd tried to make me happy, and I said that she could no more understand my happiness than a deer could understand the diet and desire of a wolf. And she said what books do I get these ideas from (that's the nastiest Mum can ever be, to accuse me of getting my ideas from books), and then she shook me and told me to stop it, that when the boy comes I mustn't do and say these things because it would frighten him and make him ill, ill like Liam. And then I could tell she felt guilty for saying that. I wanted to tell Dad that he could foster a girl.

Neither Liam nor I went to the boy's first dinner. Liam was too ill, and I couldn't sit at the table without Liam and with this boy, whom Dad told me to think of as if he'd always been my brother. And just an hour ago, I was writing here at my desk when there was a knock at the door. It was the boy, the foster boy, who comes from nowhere, from all I do not know. He said his real name was Durward, not Pierce, and that he had an even more real name that he thought he would tell me someday. He gave me this, and then he came close, innocently and not so innocently, like the innocence in dreams, the innocence that takes you by the throat, like the fear, suddenly, that the sweet dog you've known all your life will bite your face. I felt afraid, though he was kneeling at my feet like a supplicant, like the woman in that painting. But the woman was looking into the ground. He was looking into me. He has a perfect face, like the sharpest blade, a blade that would kill mercifully, kill you before you knew you were dead, kill you so subtly that you could live your whole life dead, your whole life as amazed as the evil, powerful men who die. And yet he seemed also to be offering himself to me, giving me some kind of chance. The chance was to look away, but I did not.

We went to see Liam, who was lying in bed, holding the face mask from the oxygen canister in his hand. After Durward had gone, Liam told me that when Durward had first looked at him he'd almost had an attack he'd felt so frightened, as frightened as he'd been by that terrible nightmare he'd had a few days before Durward arrived, when he'd seen the face of a boy transform into the face of a wolf. (The boy had been with him in a tent in the desert. They had no water and so were both forced to drink a sticky liquid like egg white that streamed across the floor. Dad told him that the dream was about growing up, that the boy turning into a wolf was himself turning into a man.) It seemed, Liam told me, that when Durward was looking down at him, his face was about to transform terribly. But then Durward had bent down and rested his ear gently upon Liam's chest, listening, and he'd said, "I can hear the hive of your lungs."

Later, to me, Durward said, without pity, just a little surprised, as if it were merely a strange fact, "A hive without a queen."

6

ALEX LAY NAKED on the fatman's musky bed in the heat. This was how he imagined it: a hot and humid place, like the rainforest, the Orient, where you were always sweating, purifying yourself, where everything was alive and wanted your blood, where you lay hotly alive beneath the shroud of a mosquito net. He'd closed all the doors and had switched all the heaters to full — the radiator, the little three-bar heater, and the fan heater he'd got the fatman to buy yesterday. He'd piled clothes at the base of the doors to prevent drafts, and though he had pots of water boiling on the stove there was humidity enough just from the dampness of the basement bedsit. A wavy border of green mold had risen two feet all round the walls. The trails of slugs, which came in from the garden, crisscrossed the room (he'd woken once with a trail right over the soft bellies of his eyelids). He turned facedown into the sheets, redolent of the fatman, and with an open mouth he breathed it in.

Hover above him, the boy on the bed, slender, naked, pale, sluiced with sweat, lying on his right side, his right leg straight, his left bent at the knee, his right arm tucked beneath his head, his left held out perpendicular to his body, his hand limp over the bed's edge. A kind of calligraphy, a glyph, but indecipherable, for hanging above him as you are, if you do not desire him, you do not see him. Only if you've had that lover who's had you by the root do you see him.

His hair is dyed blond, unkempt, even matted, his nose rather bony, sharp, and long for his small face, his eyes almost orientally narrow, green flecked with yellow. A small mouth (never more than a taste), its lips of such exquisite definition that in seeing them one can feel their impress. These lips could not be more evolved. Lips of stone. They are an end. His teeth are by no means perfect, the lower crowded, wayward, though the upper are strong and white. As for his chin — one might describe it even as slightly weak.

And then perhaps I'm describing my lost lover, the one remembered in my skin. Or her. Or him.

Alex had been lying on the bed for almost the entire four and a half hours since the fatman had left for work. His only activity had been to make half a dozen egg-mayonnaise sandwiches for the fatman's lunch, to run to the bakery to buy him a couple of jam doughnuts, an iced bun, and an eclair, and on the way back to get from the newsagents across the road the latest *Tales from the Crypt* and *Beyond the Grave*, which, by the light of a candle, he would read to the fatman later tonight. But now he did not read, did not watch television. For him, without people there was nothing, and he was angry at the fatman because he'd promised to be back at one, and it was now ten past one. The anger was like a small air bubble in his heart, disturbing its beat. Carefully, he sat himself up, but the old bed creaked and instantly the dog, which he'd locked outside, began to whine again and scratch at the back door.

A second later, he heard the fatman running down the concrete steps, listened to his labored breath as he frantically shoved the key into the front door. The dog whined and scratched even more desperately. The boy turned to stone.

The door seemed almost to cave inward as the fatman barreled in, burdened with shopping bags.

"I couldn't 'elp it, I couldn't 'elp it," the fatman pleaded in his own desperate defense. "Some bloke 'ad an epileptic on the bus. They 'ad to stop it." Then, to himself, high-pitched and tentative, as if making a joke of it, "Bloody 'ell, it's like the bleedin' black 'ole in 'ere. Don't know 'ow I'm goin' to pay 'lectricity."

Alex didn't move or speak. The whining of the dog redoubled.

"Ay, Feederboy," the fatman called out, putting down his shopping and moving toward the back door.

"Leave him outside," Alex said peremptorily.

The fatman gave the boy a squeamish look and again spoke as if to himself, "'E don't like being outside. Likes cump'ny." Stricken with concern, his hand now rested on the handle of the back door. "Ay, Feederboy," he whispered consolingly, but this just made the dog howl even louder. "I'll just go outside, eh? 'E won't come in. I'll just 'ave a little word with 'im, ay. 'E likes cump'ny."

But the fatman remained frozen, his hand on the handle, staring at Alex's cold, implacable, lovely face; his cold, implacable, lovely body. He glanced guiltily over at the clock on the mantel and finally returned to the shopping bags, which he brought over to the bed.

"Got you some of your favorites," the fatman said with timid placation as he sat on the bed's edge. "Cream caramel. Went to Mark-Spencer 'specially." He was wearing an old tweed coat and a trilby hat. His mouth was always open, his small, intense, bloodshot eyes always blinking. He looked horribly unhealthy and yet powerful, blood his humor, distinct red veins coursing through the flushed skin of his cheeks. He looked, as Alex often joked, as if he could kill ten grown men with his bare hands, after which he would promptly die of a heart attack. And indeed, despite his great strength, he had problems with his heart, as he did with his breathing. He was like Sisyphus, the rock his own body, the slope his own health.

Held in suspension, tentative, fearful, the fatman suckled the room's rank and humid air and tried to find with his eyes some hold upon that hard, beautiful face — the bone of the nose, the sharp relief of the lips, those narrow eyes wild, though their color, that yellow-shot green, unearthly, almost artificial.

"What time is it?" Alex said at last, his voice frigid.

"I couldn't 'elp it. This man 'ad an epileptic in the bus, didn't 'e."

"What time is it?" repeated Alex in exactly the same tone.

The fatman glanced sheepishly at the clock. "Gone one."

"What time did you say you would be here?"

"I ran. Vinny kep' me late, said I 'adn't cleaned out the changing room prop'ly."

"What time did you say you would be here?"

The dog let out another pitiful howl.

"Ay, Feederboy, ay," the fatman called soothingly but distractedly, his face evacuated by his panic. Finally he said, "One."

Now, with a reproach that betrayed some tenderness, the boy said, "I've been waiting for you."

"Got you all your favorites," the fatman said, heartened by that slight weakness in the boy's tone. "Went to Mark-Spencer 'specially. I promise I'll never be late again. I promise."

"The next time you're late," the boy said gently, implacably, "is the last time you'll ever see me."

The fatman looked stricken. "You couldn't go. Not now. Look, I got you all your favorites." The fatman quickly pulled some of the packets out of the shopping bag, throwing them onto the bed. "Mark-Spencer."

The boy didn't say anything else. The dog continued to howl.

The fatman waited for as long as he could bear and then said, "Can I let 'im in? Please . . . ? 'E don't like being on 'is own."

The boy lay back down and made a vague, languid gesture with one hand, at which the fatman shambled rapidly over to the back door and opened it.

Feederboy, a little black and white bulldog, frenziedly pushed his face into the fatman's playfully parrying hands.

He let the dog lick his face and then gave him a handful of treats from his pocket, all the time glancing back nervously at Alex, who hadn't moved. A few moments later he returned to the bed, on the end of which Feederboy also jumped.

The fatman looked over the boy's body for a moment and then rested his hand tentatively on the boy's thigh, his fingers lightly touching the clean line of a long white scar.

"I've only got twenty minutes then I got get back to work," the fatman said, his desire compressed, enclosed by his fear.

The boy sat up with such violent suddenness that the fatman snatched away his hand. The boy brought his face just a few inches from the fatman's.

"Bite your lip," the boy said quietly, but with a deadly earnestness.

The fatman looked confused.

"Bite your lip," the boy repeated.

The fatman bit gingerly at his own lip a few times, as if parodying someone in deep concentration.

"No. Bite *into* it, as if it's a piece of meat, something not attached to you, something you're going to eat."

The fatman swallowed hard, hardly able to look at that cold, adamant face. But the more firmly he clenched his lower lip between his teeth, the more real that face seemed. And suddenly there were streams of blood running down his chin, dripping down onto the boy's chest and stomach, and just like a stone face, or one's own face in the mirror, or the face of a corpse if one stares into it for long enough, the boy's face came to life.

41

7

DURWARD HAS SO MUCH PATIENCE, spends a lot of time with Liam, reading to him, playing games. Both Dad and Mum love Durward. He charms Mum in the way that men try to do when we have parties. His style is the same and she responds to him in the same way, coyly — even though he's only a boy. And for Dad he's perfect <u>because</u> he's perfect. Everything that Dad teaches him, he learns, learns so quickly, and as he watches or reads, or seems to see something new in you, or wishes to take his understanding of you to another level, he becomes entirely absorbent, porous, in the way that very young children do. His mouth slackens, his eyes empty. Learning to play football for Dad, he watched a game on the television, and it was as if he were entranced, only every now and then lifting his hand to touch his lips in that way of his. But unlike me, he cannot be alone. At first this irritated me, but not now. Now, if he's away, I miss him. I find myself waiting, vacantly, for the front door to open, for the sound of his voice. And, like me, he has his darkness, that terrible darkness that descends upon him. I've found him shaking and white, as if he has a fever, and then he wants no one. This happens if Dad gets angry or disappointed in him — one time when Durward had exhausted Liam too much, bringing on an attack; another when he missed a vital penalty for the school football team. It's as if he can hardly bring himself to breathe. He loves Dad more than anyone. Thank God Dad does not know that sometimes Durward insists on taking Liam outside with us, even as far as the woods and the lake, once as far as the quarry. This frightens me, and often Liam has been at the edge of an attack while we've been far from home. But Durward says that it's no life to lie in bed; better to die in the woods, near water. Liam loves Durward too, and it's incredible, looking at them both together, to think that they are the same age. Durward is as tall as I am, and when he goes naked to swim in the lake, I find it hard to look innocently at him. Last time we went I had my period, so I didn't go into the water, but sat on the bank. He called to me, but I refused. Then he came out of the water, emerged with not a thought of his nakedness, for in a way he's always naked. He stood in front of me. I couldn't look at him. Then he squatted down. "Are you bleeding?" he said. I nodded. I thought he was returning to the water, but he went to his trousers and opened the small penknife he keeps on his key ring. Before I could stop him he made a long cut on the inside of his thigh. In a stream his blood ran down his leg, and he held his hand out to me.

8

SEAN STOPPED HIS CAR and in his side mirror watched the child running up to the door. The boy got in and quickly surveyed Sean's face. This was the seventh boy Sean had picked up. He felt as if some of the others had recognized the photograph, but even when he'd raised his offer to five hundred pounds they wouldn't help him. This one looked the youngest so far, perhaps twelve or thirteen, but with the body of a skinny eight-year-old, his head and eyes too large. He had a cold sore just beneath his nose.

"I'm looking for someone," Sean said as he drove off. "I'll pay you ten pounds now for your time, and if you can help me find him, I'll pay you three hundred."

He handed the boy the photograph of Pierce.

"He might have blond hair now, and he's older, about two years older. He was renting here a few months ago. I knew him as Pierce, but he might also call himself Tobias, Devon, or Durward — anything."

"What's 'e done?" the little boy said in an affectedly

tough, but rather high-pitched voice, his rodent-like mouth pursing.

"He's not done anything. I'm not the police."

"'E giy ya a gobbler you couldn't forget?" the boy said, for some reason parodying a Scottish accent. He giggled and suddenly frowned. Delicately, unconsciously, he dabbed his finger on the scabbed sore beneath his nose.

Sean couldn't stop looking at the little boy's hands, the long and filthy nails. He smelled musky, sweaty, and an odor of mothballs emanated from an enormous old cardigan he was wearing, the pockets of which bulged with wads of tissue paper.

"Would you mind putting on your seat belt?" Sean said.

The boy giggled again, this time nervously. He pulled the seat belt over him, but couldn't get the end into the latch. Sean reached down to help, but as his hand touched the boy's, something in him recoiled and he flinched away. The boy removed his own hand, blushing, and let Sean do it for him.

"I once went through the winda," the boy said, somewhat apologetically. "In my mum's car."

Sean nodded.

The boy went on: "My mum's a beautician works for the BBC she did Marti Cane one time and also Miss Slocum from *Are You Being Served?* and she said they was really nice." The boy spoke in a flat, rapid, unarticulated stream. "Only famous person I seen was Russ Abbot an' 'e was really tall."

Sean said nothing. The boy dabbed again at his cold sore.

45

"'Ow much you gonna to give me?" the boy said.

"Ten pounds now," Sean repeated. "Three hundred if you help me find him."

"That's Priestly."

"So you know him?" Sean could hardly subdue the sudden edge of desperation in his voice, but this boy was either not canny or not experienced enough to take advantage of it.

"'E's all right, Priestly. 'E 'elped me out when I first come. I got into a car that 'ad stopped for another kid and when I got back they was waitin' for me. 'E stopped 'em from kickin' the shit out of me and 'e 'elped me out, told me what to do, 'ow much to ask for, and some of the cars I shouldn't get into. All the boys like 'im; only boy didn't like 'im was Mumford 'e wanted to fight 'im 'cos Mumford like thinks 'e's like really 'ard, and Mumford 'ad a knife right, and Mumford 'ad 'is knife out right, and Priestly don't seem scared at all, and Priestly don't seem 'ard right though I know 'e's really 'ard 'cos 'e can beat Batty at mercy and I seen 'im 'ave a fight once wiv a skin'ead who called 'im a shitsticker and 'e fuckin' duffed 'im but 'e didn't 'ave a knife, but Mumford was a bit scared 'cos the other boys really like Priestly, 'cos 'e 'elps 'em out right and 'cos 'e's really funny, and 'e makes us all feel like we're like this business or summin'" (now the boy had started to smile, abstracted, remembering), "and 'e makes us call the dicks 'clients' our 'clients' and 'e goes right up to Mumford right, not even looking at the knife, and we fink 'e's going to start fighting, but 'e suddenly goes into this routine, and-and-

and 'e starts becoming each one of us right, and does this
thing, like the knife's a cock right, and 'e's doin' me, like I
won't give the guy a gobbler 'cos I'm tellin' 'im 'bout my
mum like knowing all these famous people right, 'cos I talk
quite a lot 'bout my mum, they-they say I talk too much, so
'e pretends 'e's me, and then 'e does Baxter" (the boy was
giggling now, and stammering breathlessly) "who's this like
complete bitch queen right, with this client we call Tar-
zan 'cos he likes to touch us up while 'e's listening to this
tape of like monkeys chattering, and birds, and like jungle
sounds. And Mumford doesn't know what to do, and 'e's
like laughing 'imself, and then-and then-and then Priestly
does this impression of 'im, of Mumford, wiv 'is knife,
an' the way 'e talks, like 'I'm goin' to fuck you up man,'
And like so we're all laughing at 'im, an' even Mumford's
laughin', 'cos 'e was laughing already, and the only one's
not laughing is Priestly. 'E's smiling. 'E smiles a lot, and 'e's
looking at Mumford, but 'e's not laughin'. 'E never laughs,
Priestly. 'E never laughs."

Sean could see it, could see Pierce's face; no, he never
laughed, smiled yes, gave you more than a laugh sometimes, a look as if he were almost too amazed or awed to
laugh at your wit. Sean could see that beautiful, fearless
face, staring into the now truckling features of the thug
who'd challenged his supremacy, this Mumford with his
knife, who Pierce had placed into an arena of laughing
faces, forcing him to laugh at his own grotesque parody, to
participate in his own humiliation, the knife in his hand
now the very font of his effacement, his utter defeat. And

despite himself, despite everything, like a thin armature of hot wire within the frigid corpus of all his rage, Sean felt pride.

"So do you know where I can find him?" Sean said.

The boy frowned and looked deeply concerned: "Like if I 'elp you find 'im, will you give me the three 'undred in like small notes, like fivers."

"Yes, yes, of course."

"I know 'e's wiv the fatman."

"Who?"

"The fatman. 'E's like this client. 'E's all right. 'E 'as this big gray Bedford."

"So Priestly's living with him?"

"I 'eard that. Somewhere 'round Tower 'amlets I fink 'e lives."

"And what does he look like, this man?"

The boy giggled. "'E's fat."

"I mean how would I know him if I saw him — apart from him being fat?"

"'E's *fat* and 'e's got a red face and 'e 'as a little dog with 'im sometimes, a little bulldog, black and white one. And Priestly does come 'ere sometimes to see us, mostly to see Vin and Mick, Sat'day, Sunday, 'e comes sometimes. The fatman brings 'im in 'is van."

Sean drove the boy back to where he'd picked him up.

The boy undid the seat belt with both hands, and then looked at Sean with his over-large eyes as Sean reached for his wallet.

"So if you find 'im you're goin' to give me the three 'undred quid?"

"Yes. I'll come back and I'll give it to you."

The boy seemed a little troubled again, dabbing at his sore.

"If I find him within the next two weeks," Sean reassured him, "I'll come back here on Sunday at eight o'clock."

"Right 'ere?" the boy said, pointing into the ground.

"Right here."

He handed the boy twenty pounds.

"I ain't got no change," the boy said with an affected aggressiveness, snatching the note.

Sean just waved his hand.

"Fanks, mate," the boy said, getting out, his eyes widening even further with forgetfully innocent gratitude.

"And if you get any more information," Sean said, handing the boy a piece of paper with his address on it, "this is where I'm staying. It's a boat on the river near the power station."

After the boy had shut the car door, Sean drove straight to a chemist. He bought two boxes of antiseptic wipes with which he cleaned his hands and everything the boy had touched.

9

THIS TIME the dream was not a dream but his cool hand against her cheek. He was hunched over in the darkness. Theresa switched on the lamp beside her bed and saw that his T-shirt was soaked with blood. He was holding his hand to what was obviously a wound in his side.

"What have you done?" she said, panicked, sitting bolt upright.

He said nothing, merely stared down at her, his body trembling, his expression troubled and contrite.

After getting out of her bed she helped him down onto it. She fetched the first-aid kit from the bathroom, pulled off his T-shirt, and dressed the long but thankfully shallow cut just to the left of his navel. He was wearing a pair of jean cutoffs and scuffed white plimsolls. The latter she also removed.

"We should get you to a hospital," she whispered. "What happened to you?"

But he just closed his eyes as if he were going to sleep.

She was kneeling on the bed beside him, leaning over his

face, those boy's lips, his white neck, white smooth body. She could smell a kind of adult musk rising from him, redolent of everything she'd never entered, an odor like a tarnish upon the scent of the child. She could barely believe he was here. During his absence she'd been hardly living. At times she'd gone numb, completely numb, lying on her bed sobbing for hours. She'd not even been able to pray, because she couldn't bring herself to feel anything beyond her desire for his return. Since he'd left, the part of her that had been quick in God, her life, had hardened into an idol: the crucifix upon her wall. That agonized Christ, in all his constriction and collapse, once freeing her, raising her, had now become a thing merely of steel, stamped out in a factory, a God as yieldless as His own cast.

And though it had only been three months, she'd begun to feel as if Devon were dead, had kept seeing him in the street, hearing his voice, as one does with the dead. And her body didn't know what to do with the way she felt, because she'd not felt anything like it since she'd become enamored of God as a girl during her father's pilgrimage, that haze of passion and faith that had caused her to join Our Sisters of the Holy Novena a month after her father's death, that had kept her afloat as the vast ruined hulk of his life had sunk beneath her waters. Here he was now, this boy, with a face that expressed a desperate innocence, this boy who, it seemed to her, had entered every sin to emerge always inviolate and bewildered, who was so full of God as to be repelled by God — as those empty of God were drawn to Him and to the boy. And the boy was as unconscious of this, the depth of his spirit, as he was of his own beauty, of the desire he invoked in others. In him she saw her own redemption, and beyond him the terror of her life as it was, like rubbish blown along an empty street at night, nothing, ten years in a nunnery, ten years for her faith to dwindle with all the human pettiness of the nuns, ten years for the flame of her youthful passion for God to be snuffed. And then ten more years in an unconsummated marriage, looking after boys who became indistinguishable, who'd gone on and left her older, who'd swept ever more swiftly by her, eroding her heart, making it as smooth as a riverstone, a debacle of small, reaching hands, snatching with them her years. Until this boy, who had entered her room timidly one night, expressing his fears that he could not love, just a child, fearing this, telling her that he could not get a hold, that he kept slipping away, falling, as in a dream, from untenable place to untenable place, desperate, fearing that one day he would hit the earth.

His eyes opened and settled upon her, green-yellow eyes, slender, lovely, unreal.

"What happened to you?" she said.

"I got picked up," he said, "by a man in a blue van. He seemed all right." The boy paused, frowning. "He asked me to go into the back of the van with him."

"Why do you do these things?" Theresa couldn't help herself. "Why are you always trying to hurt yourself? Why don't you come back here? You could live here again."

But the boy just continued, softly, as if she hadn't said anything.

"When he opened up the back of the van, I saw that there was another man in there, an old bloke, must have been about seventy. So I tried to get away, but the first man took hold of me, shoved me in — he was a big bloke — and then the old one got a knife on me." The boy paused again, still troubled and amazed, as if it were too soon for the telling, as if the event itself might still be happening, as in dreams when one escapes, but never quite escapes. But then it was only in the telling that he could wake himself.

"They had to be really quick," the boy went on, "because we were at the end of this dead-end street, and every now and then cars would go by on the main road. I don't think anyone could really see us, but the young bloke — wasn't young really, could have been forty, fifty, I don't know — but he was shitting himself. And then he shuts the van door behind him. But with the door closed it's pitch-black in the van, so he has to open it again. And then he asks the other bloke where the torch is, and the old man tells him it's in this big bag by the door. And the bloke gets the torch out and switches it on, but it doesn't work, so he screams at the old man, and the old man starts shouting back, 'We'll take him somewhere, We'll take him some-where,' and tells him there's rope in the bag. And then the other one pulls this ball of string out of the bag. It's like a brand new ball of packaging string, and he unwraps it, but it's really thin, and he can just snap it in his hands; he looks like he's going to kill the old bloke, but the old bloke tells him he just has to wrap it round a few times and it'll hold me. And then an ambulance goes by on the main road and the younger bloke gets panicked again because I'm on the side of the van where the door's open, and he shouts at the old bloke to get me on the other side as he's unwinding the string. And I knew then I had to take my chance. And I'd seen this screwdriver lying on the floor beside the bag; so I kick the old man in his stomach — that's when he got me with the knife, just when he was falling back — and the other bloke pulls the door shut to stop me from getting out. So it's pitch-black, but I'd fixed it in my head, where the screwdriver was, and I dived on the floor and got it, and then I felt the younger bloke take hold of me. He was so fucking strong, suffocating me. Like being buried alive. But I got my hand free, then I got him with the screwdriver, as hard as I could. In the stomach. And when I got him with the screwdriver he shouted, 'Dad, Dad.' Screamed it. He screamed it. The old bloke was his dad." More slowly, quietly, the boy said, "I think I killed him. It went right into him, the screwdriver. And I shoved him over to where his dad was and I got out; and I ran to the main road and I looked back; and the van door was open, but no one came out of it. I think I killed him."

She said nothing for a while, kneeling beside his body on the bed, looking down at that face, which was turned away from her now, lost in thought, a face that emptied her and so made of her a temple, like all empty things, like deserts and dereliction, like the eyes of infants and zealots.

Holy face, those lips, almost overwrought, sensual and sophisticated, but forged in the most extreme naiveté; that slender crag of a nose, which threw his mouth and eyes into

even more delicate relief. He came to her because he believed her to be good, believed she could help him find some
less frenetic way to feel, help him love "God or just something steady," he'd once said. Came to her because she
would love him not through her body or mind but through
her God. Here, his suffering, supine figure, helpless, for-
saken. He'd come to her for help, but it was he who'd
returned her to God, who'd imbued her God with life
again, with his life, who'd made tumid once more those
visceral roots of faith. And was this not him, his terrible
fate, that in all his tragic and uncomprehended loveliness,
the pure goodness and innocence of his heart amid that
welter of sin, this boy beloved of sin, that amid all of this,
just the sight of him gave her a kind of faith. His goodness
was so volatile because it was so pure. She wanted to kiss
his lips. That was the impulse of her admixture of sin, to
kiss God, to kiss God. But to kiss God is to betray him.

She put her gaunt hand upon his face, cupping his cheek,
and his eyes, intensely slender, turned upon her, unreal eyes
like a gift or an affliction.

"We'll pray to God," she said.

He glanced up at the steel crucifix, directly above his
head on the wall.

"After what He did to His son?" he retorted, his tone
sardonic.

"He *is* His own son. I've told you that. I've told you that
a hundred times."

A slightly cruel smile now ghosted his lips.

"I feel for Him in a way," he said almost blithely, as if

musing to himself. "You see, He had no father — biologically, I mean — which is hard for a kid, because it's not hard, by which I mean that He cannot harden. Thing is, He could have had one of mine. I have so many fathers I barely know what to do with them."

"But He had a father. He *was* His father," she repeated with heat.

"Had or has? Was or is?" he said, regarding her with an enigmatic speculation.

"Has, is."

But his eyes had turned back up to the crucifix even before she'd replied, and he was now smiling as if remembering something. Rhythmically, maintaining that smile, and with increasing volume he intoned: "A great scum of fathers upon the face of the waters, a rotting glut of fathers, a great steaming mound of fathers." He almost shouted this last phrase, the words seeming to make him deliriously happy.

"Shhhh," she said, placing her hand upon his lips, afraid that he would be heard.

But he tore his face angrily away and loudly continued: "And I killed one of them today, shoved that fucking thing right into his gut." He caught his breath and looked, just for a moment, as if he were going to cry, before whispering, "I've gone too far."

"You haven't," Theresa said, placing her hands on his naked shoulders, straddling him with her arms. "You don't know you killed him."

He closed his eyes, and though his face went completely

still, his anguish seemed to rise to the surface and harden on contact with the air, becoming masklike.

"I've gone too far," he repeated through the mouthpiece of this mask, and in his voice there was something so terrible, hopeless, and final, it wrenched her heart.

"You can't go too far for God, for redemption," she exhorted him. "There is no sin — "

"Well, *He*'s not going far, is He?" the boy cut her off, his eyes opening upon the crucifix again. Instantly his anguish broke, fell away, his face calm, renewed, his manner matter-of-fact, "Your bird up there. Someone should tell him that you need some flexibility to fly, some suppleness of soul. But his soul is that cross; it always was, poor kid. His father was a carpenter. He didn't want a son, he wanted a cross, one with a perfect dovetail at the transept — the dovetail of the Holy Ghost."

"Stop it," Theresa hissed. "You're not making any sense." Her small hands had gone white with the pressure. She was pushing him down into the bed, and he was looking up at her with an amused amazement.

But all at once his expression became utterly serious: "I have known God," he said firmly, softly, feelingly. And then, "Is this in the Bible, 'I have sweated with His lustful ghost'? I have sweated with His lustful ghost," he repeated louder. "It should be. For me, God is a heavy man. He's on top of me and he smells — what was it that man in that van smelled of? I remember it because I thought, if I'm going to die, I want to remember it. You know what he smelled of? He smelled of England. He smelled of condensed milk and canned peaches and margarine on white bread with just the ghost of a slice of ham upon it and a tasteless paste of mustard. Tasteless *paste* of mustard," he repeated, as if he just liked the sound of it. "And it was so intimate when I killed him. And it was just the weight of him, like being buried alive, the weight of God. It's like being buried alive. I just wanted to *get him off me.*" He shouted these last words furiously, his eyes fixing upon her.

She took her hands off his shoulders.

They both remained silent for a long while, perhaps ten minutes.

Finally she said, "But you're so good."

"That's why they come back, sweetheart," he said in a deep camp voice, that smile that was more than laughter breaking over his lips.

"No, no you *are,*" she said with pathetic insistence. "All the boys here, they adored you. When you were here everything was so different. Now they're like old men who've had their lives. They just talk about when you were here. They talk about you all the time. At dinner it's just one story after another about how funny you were, how strong you were, how fair you were, how clever you were," she said. "And you stopped all their vicious pettiness. Even that boy who had a stutter. What was his name?"

"Malcolm."

"Yes. Malcolm. Everyone hated him. Everyone made fun of him. Except you. You didn't hate anyone. I've never seen you hate anyone. And it was you who stopped him from stuttering."

"Hallelujah," the boy cut in cynically, "and they brought to him the child with the p-p-p-persistent p-p-p-plosives, and — "

"You're good to everyone," she stubbornly continued. "You're incorrigibly good — to everyone."

"Not everyone," he said with an enigmatic vindictiveness.

She was so desperate to know what he thought, what he felt, but in all his searing honesty there was not one thing he gave away; in his naked face, not one thing he exposed.

She wanted to hold him down again, to pinion him, to keep him here, to keep him with her.

"Daniel has been heartbroken since you left," she said.

Now she had got through to him. He winced, and she was glad.

"How is he?"

"Heartbroken," she repeated emphatically.

The boy frowned and looked angry, frustrated for a moment. Abruptly he reached into his pocket and pulled out a handful of crumpled notes, like so much rubbish. He pushed them into her hands.

"Will you do something for me?" he said. "Will you buy him a model of a Stuka? It's a German dive bomber. There's one in the window of the Sunshine Shop. And also get him a pound of Licorice Allsorts, but take out all of those blue and pink jelly ones." He put his hand gently on her shoulder. "I know that's a lot of trouble, but it's a sort of private joke. He'll understand it. Put it in his room when he's not there."

She was unraveling the notes, most of them twenties and tens.

"This is over a hundred pounds," she said. Suddenly a strange, unpleasant thrill pulsed through her, as she thought of where this money had come from, under what circumstances it had changed hands.

He wasn't listening.

"You need this money," she said, thrusting it toward him. "I'll buy Daniel the things."

But he wouldn't even look at the money, just said, frowning as if annoyed he even had to think about it, "If there's money left buy something else, buy something for the house."

Then she remembered: "There's someone looking for you."

"Who?"

"A Mr. Hennessy."

It was a shock, a genuine shock in his face, which Theresa, starving for any sign that she could deeply touch him, fed upon as she had upon his guilt about Daniel.

After a while, he said, "What did you tell him?"

"I said I didn't know where you were, which I don't. Caitlín says he's living on her boat now."

"On her boat?" The boy smiled sadly and let out a groan of despair. "He's living on Caitlín's boat? *Oh God,* how sad. Theresa, do you know why the devil is so bad?" The boy was suddenly angry, impatient. "He's so bad because his job is so fucking easy. He could be redeemed in a day if he could just make one evil thing. Just one. If he could actually make it and not have to watch it make itself in front of him. It's *quality*, not quantity; why will God never understand that?"

Theresa looked down at him, perplexed and contrite, though she didn't really know what he was talking about.

"Did he seem pretty determined to find me?"

"He did. He said he'd fostered you."

"Yes . . ." The boy looked thoughtful. "He was my father for a while, and I have a feeling he was the Sean Hennessy my mother met through the social services. He was her caseworker and took, indeed, a great deal of interest in every item of her personal luggage — as many men did with my mother, being that she was a six-year-old child in the body of a very attractive woman. Actually he's the prime candidate for my real father — perhaps I should say the incumbent. He's one of the two dozen or so men my mother claimed it could very likely have been. He was the only one of them, in fact, whose full, real name I actually know, because one time my mother used a whole bunch of social service documents to fill in a hole in the wall. I knocked out all the Polyfiller and removed that treasure of documents, one of which had on it a name — an actual name — in black and white."

"But I thought you said that your mother — "

He put his hand quickly to her lips. "Sh-sh-sh-sh-sh-sh," he said. "If my father can be every man who turns his head when he sees a pair of legs, then you've got to give me a bit of leeway with my mother. At the moment all CV's, including Mr. Hennessy's, are still under consideration."

Once more they fell into silence. Theresa couldn't move or speak. Helpless. He did this to her, drew out that will woven through her limbs, drew it out as one could imagine one's whole system of veins or nerves being drawn out in one long, careful thread.

She saw a tremor in his face, and suddenly remembered — yes, had actually forgotten — what had just happened to the boy, so fogged was she by him.

He lifted his hand to her cheek, gently cupping it, and brought all his beauty to bear so completely, as only he could.

"I'm sorry," he said. "I'm cruel to you because you're the only person I've ever needed, the only person — adult — I know who's really good."

"I'm not good," she said meekly, feeling sick.

"You *are* good. And you have faith. And even if I can't have faith it helps me to be with you. You have something other than this life. You don't need anything from anyone. I've always been with people who've needed something from me. You don't know how many times I've wanted to come to you, Theresa. You're the only peace I have. *You're the only peace I have.* When I think of you, thinking of God, it gives me peace — vicarious perhaps, but it is peace. If I can't sleep, which is often, I imagine you, here on your bed, praying. What I mean is . . . is that your desire transcends those desires in which all the people I know are mired. And in which I'm mired too. You're good to me, but you don't *need* me. And your love for me is of the same substance as your love for anyone else."

He went silent again, for a long while, looking away from her, but his hand still against her cheek. Then, softly, as if to himself, he said, "Maybe I didn't kill him."

His hand was trembling. She steadied it against her face. Her head felt numb, the beat of her heart painful, spongy, too full of him to think about what he'd done.

Withdrawing his hand, he got up off the bed, said something to her about borrowing one of her white shirts. And then he was gone, and she was left still kneeling on her bed, but now facing the open window, her back to the crucifix; and the room was empty, had emptied out into the night. Kneeling toward his bloody T-shirt, which hung over the end of her bed, a gaunt, inviolate woman, racked, the hard, yellowed soles of her feet, the hollows of her face, blue veins prominent in her thin arms. She lifted her hands, resting them in her lap, and, looking down, she saw that they were full of money.

10

DURWARD SAID NOTHING to me when I got back from the hospital last night, by which I mean that he did not admonish me or ask me questions about why I had cut my arms — as I know Mum and Dad must have asked him to. And what could I say? My arms felt as heavy as storm clouds; I wanted them to rain? What could I say? I did it because I could not feel anything, because my skin was too tight and my blood couldn't breathe? What could I say? That there is a kernel of spiritual euphoria in this numb sadness?

Lying in bed that night, I could hear Mum crying and Dad's muffled voice, muffling voice, stifling voice. She wants to take me to see a psychologist, but Dad refuses. He's devouring books on psychology. He wants to fix me himself, as if I were a washing machine. And if he fixes me, I can keep cleaning all the dirty laundry of the past. From the past comes all the badness to me, all that's not said to

64

children, the sins of my genealogy. It's no one's fault. Durward told me that I was an innocence racked with past sins. But this sin has to live somewhere and is as vital as it is virulent.

Dad will never understand the heaviness in me, the voluptuous weight, which Durward can, if he chooses, consummate. Sometimes, as I'm sinking down, he'll decide to pull me out, sing songs from musicals to me. My favorite is the one from *My Fair Lady*. But more often he lowers me in. Perhaps it's because he knows I will go anyway. And he will sing me that song:

> I dreamed I were so great for her.
> That I was only me she dreamed.
> I dreamed for her I lived forever.
> She dreamed me dead to deepen love.
> So I dreamed myself a monument,
> And dead indeed with silent face,
> So she might suffer constantly —
> But Constant was she not to me,
> And another loves she now.

Last night he came into my room and got into my bed, pulling himself up behind me. I tried to turn around to him, but he wouldn't let me. We talked for a while, softly in the darkness. I told him that I just felt dead sometimes, but that it was not always bad, and that's what people didn't understand. He said he did understand, and that he and I were of the same element. He talked about Keats, how Keats had died at twenty-five of TB after seeing both his mother and brother die of the same disease. He recited to me — no, sang to me, "Ode to a Nightingale." I could feel his breath, sometimes even his lips at the back of my neck. He said that we would not live much longer, he and I, that he would not become a man. It made me think of the boy-man's body emerging from the lake, sluiced with the sunlight coming through the trees, the boy's body, impermeably naked, reflecting that light, while the man's absorbed it. He whispered a verse again, something like — "I have been half in love with easeful Death, take into the air my quiet breath. It's rich to die." Then he recited one of the last poems Keats wrote, as he lay dying — "This living hand, in the icy silence of the tomb, I hold it towards you." He told me that Keats was in love with a woman called Fanny Brawne, a woman he could not touch because of his sickness, that though she lived in the house next door to his, they had to correspond by letters, and that every day, at an appointed hour, he would watch her walk past his window. Durward had a book with him of Keats' love letters to her; and he read one of them to me. It was so full of longing, so beautiful. It was better even than the poems. I cried. And as I cried, he sang to me again that song of his, medieval, lilting, far away. I felt myself going numb, going dead as his hands moved slowly down my arms, over the bandages, and coupled with mine, his song a spiraling thread of light in a well of darkness, as if he were dropping stars into me. And then he told me his real name, the name I could never write down and never say again, the name he'd only ever revealed to me. And then he said that he'd told me a lie, that the letter he'd read had not been written by Keats to Fanny Brawne, but by him. To me.

11

SEAN RETURNED to the boat after another day spent driving around Victoria. Out on the deck sat three of its seemingly numberless tenants, college students barely out of their teens. A sluggish, bovine boy with enormous bare feet strummed hopelessly at a guitar for two ethereal girls, one of whom was plaiting the gold-blonde hair of the other into cornrows. Embarrassed, Sean passed them with a curt nod. The girls giggled as he entered the boat.

The main cabin, which contained the communal kitchen and sitting room, reeked of damp and marijuana. There were a couple of ragged, moldy couches, so many guitars it seemed they were breeding, and about three dozen coffee cups, in some of which the mold had scaled enough avatars to be considered houseplants. Worse still, he could see the droppings of rats on the gas stove.

He leaned against the kitchen counter, watched a barge pass by on the Thames, and succumbed to a heavy sadness. He closed his eyes, lulled by the boat's rocking in the barge's wake, and felt, wanted desperately to feel, that he could open them into his youth, that by some instinct called up by the sheer extent of his own incredulity at where his life had brought him, he could find his way back through the labyrinth of these past twenty-five years into the light of day.

But almost at once something in him revolted at this weakness. All his life — except for that one incident — he'd been so strong, had never understood weakness, laziness, depression. This strength he'd got from his mother — her arid, desolate strength. She'd never revealed anything about her past, but Sean's father had once told him that she'd come from real poverty. The oldest of thirteen children, living in the East End of London, her father, an Irish laborer, had been killed after scaffolding had collapsed beneath him. So she and her mother, with what supplementary benefit they could get, had become a taut membrane about that vast family, those twelve children struggling to grow up, to shed them. Sean didn't even know the names of his mother's brothers and sisters, and couldn't ask her because he was afraid, more for himself than for her, to broach her silence. Afraid most of that other thing his father had mentioned — without any details because his father didn't know any — that there had been some event, some shame or outrage that had caused Sean's mother to break off all contact with her family. Something appalling, unforgivable, had happened, about which, now that she was dead, Sean would never know.

As a boy, Sean could hardly remember ever seeing his mother sit down or eat. She would drink cups of strong, black tea standing in the kitchen, her eyes shifting restlessly

over all the things she'd already cleaned. While he ate her
stodgy meals, she would stand by the table looking down at
him, her face the face of one who had suffered and sur-
vived, was still suffering, surviving some great hunger, one
arm slung horizontally across her waist, the other vertical,
holding a cigarette at her hard cheek. Yes, there was something atavistic about her. She was not really watching him,
her only child, but was watching still those twelve other
children from that former life, to which she'd given too
much of herself to ever escape, those twelve needy children
about which she was still wound, stretched to translucence.
Sean could see them in her eyes, estranged from her by that
secret, the unforgivable thing, of which he came to feel
himself the incarnation, the embodiment of silence, of guilt
or outrage. So it was he who mediated those twelve children. He was the vessel through which they were invoked
by his mother's eyes, and within the solipsism of the single
child, Sean gave them names, personalities, histories.

Sean's own father was at home so rarely, intruded upon
their lives with his largesse like a bachelor uncle into the
lives of his brother's widow and child. He had about him
that dense mystery of men, men making deals in the arcane
world of the pubs, buying and selling truckloads of goods
that had gone awry from the manufacturers, dealing in
cash, the trust of a few drinks, and a firm handshake. He
was a gambler, as all true men are, never thinking of security, each deal like diving off a cliff with just a glimpse of
blue water among all the rocks below you, gravity gone, all
the pressure of air in your lungs, your life in that exhilara-

tion in your chest, in streamlining yourself as you fall. In those rare visits to the house, bringing toys and wads of cash, he would pull Sean up onto his knees and tell him — his eyes bloodshot, his nose and cheeks red-veined and flushed, the alcohol so pungent on his breath — tell him about his future deals, that if he could just pull off this next one, they would be rolling in clover for the rest of their lives. But this was spoken in passing, for he was always falling: Sean could feel it in the frantic beat of his father's heart, see it in the wild exhilaration of his eyes, searching somewhere below him for that speck of blue. He would scrutinize all his father's expressions, gestures, and motions, trying to fathom him from the outside in, finally understanding that to be a man meant that one never made any physical errors, one never spilled or dropped anything, one never took a false step, and one clad oneself in the iron of a dry, laconic humor. Yes, Sean had absorbed his father in these periodic intrusions up until he was thirteen years old, after which his father never returned to the house, and Sean only ever saw him again once more in his life.

Sean now looked out at those young girls on the deck, the sadness in him like some enfeebled creature with black wings it had not strength enough even to lift, and thought of his wife. His wife — of whom Caitlín reminded him so acutely — had seemed lost and fragile, irrational and romantic, though not affectedly so. That would never have attracted him. And if he'd suggested these things to her, it would have made her furious. He'd loved her as something inconceivable. He'd loved her sudden emotion, expressed in fits of temper or affection, had loved the fact that she wanted memories, that she harvested and preserved the present. Spontaneously, she would decree special days and special dinners, stills in time, in which the point was to hold off, as long as possible, the next day. All of this had been so incomprehensible to him, though he did understand it to be life, and coveted it, coveted her. But for him each day existed purely for the next, and such voluptuous stillness made him only anxious.

He had loved her, had loved her body, her honest sensuality, her eyes, her face, her hair — and yes, it was possession, though he was rarely jealous, for she required a leap of faith, faith in her love for him, which he had taken. Almost.

She was the genius of his love, its perfect expression — beyond him, for inside him, between the desolate mother and the falling father, there was no place for it. And it is when our lives live beyond us that we become vulnerable and desperate. Even after years of marriage, his stomach would knot if he ever saw her when she wasn't aware that he was watching, saw her nursing their children or sitting alone and abstracted in the garden. My life, he would think. Yet she was the part of him that needed to be out of his control. She was the falling of his father, that exhilarating pressure in his lungs. Or perhaps he'd loved her most because he'd never quite believed in her. When she'd been gone from the house, she'd seemed utterly gone, impossible — either in the present and present completely, or irrevocably past, mere memory. Each time he'd touched her, there had been something empirical in it.

But now she was gone. He wondered where, and if she was with someone else. Wondered also, as always, why, with just that single letter to say that she could not stay, that he must not seek her out. Of course she was traumatized, but could she blame him for what had happened?

She was gone and he was looking for the boy, the boy who had sabotaged his life, the boy who was perhaps his son, the boy who was that one mistake in a life that was to have been perfect, unimpeachable.

Sean had been a young man of twenty-two on his first job as a qualified caseworker. This job was an important step in the plan he'd laid out for his life. He was subject to a consuming ambition. From where this ambition had come, his mother's famine, his father's falling, he didn't know. But early in his life he resolved to enter (carrying within the shell of his father, as most men do, the shameful secret of his mother) that most arcane and exclusive of men's clubs, the government. More than that, he determined to head the government. His father desired only to fall, but Sean wished to ascend, to achieve that elevation at which he could tell wonderful lies to his children about the deals he was making, about that time when they would all roll in clover.

Sean conceived of himself as the head of his country, the perfect man. And of course, this would be a vast subterfuge, for he knew himself to be a man of no substance, a brief weight upon his father's legs, the twelve ghostly children his mother served food to, a subterfuge, but one pushed so far it would become substantial. For that had been his early realization: that the real was just subterfuge precipitated in time, as stars precipitate in space and become, by virtue of distance, perspective, and imagination, constellations. Yes, that's what he'd learned from the wedding.

It was the wedding of Lance, his best friend at school, getting married at just sixteen to Melany. Sean was the best man. It was at a large Catholic church in North London. After the ceremony, the photographer took pictures of the entire congregation crowded on the long flight of marble steps that led up to the church's vast doorway. When all the photographs were over, the bride and groom, in showers of shouting and rice, began to descend the stairs toward the waiting Rolls Royce, the door of which was being held open by the chauffeur. But the two newlyweds pulled up short as a derelict man staggered into the space between them and the open door.

It was a miracle the man could stand, his whole body swaying like something inanimate in the wind. His hair was greasy, matted, and he held, by its neck, a liter bottle of red wine. Everyone in the congregation went quiet, froze. Suddenly the bottle slipped out of the derelict's hand and smashed upon the pavement. He surveyed for a moment the mess of shattered glass, the red wine streaming away, then fell to his hands and knees and began to lap up the rivulets of wine that had formed in the cracks between the paving stones. Both his hands and knees were cut by the glass.

Melany began to cry. Sean hurried down with Lance and

a couple of other men to move the derelict away. And that was it. That was the last time Sean ever saw his father, helping to lift him from the pavement, hefting him like a sack of flour against some iron railings, then turning his back upon him as he watched the bride catch up the hem of her wedding dress to ford those rivulets of wine and blood.

Yes, perhaps that had been the seed of the resolution that had grown in Sean that he would become the idea of himself to so many children sitting upon his knees, that he would be the enigma, the pithy statements, the moments of passion, the glimpses of humanity of a distant biography. He would make a legend of his own subterfuge.

He'd mapped it all out. He was to be a man of the people, the first prime minister not to come from the old school — because he needed to make it difficult, because there was no middle ground, just perfection or ruination.

So he applied to both Oxford and Cambridge just to turn them down when they accepted him, and went instead to Birmingham University, where he studied political science. There, he was elected student president and chair of the debating society. For every current event he painstakingly wrote political speeches, which he would orate at speaker's corner every Sunday morning to develop his rhetorical style. He studied constantly — law, economics, every intricacy of government, every relevant aspect of history. He read the biographies of great statesmen, and even in his head, at times, wrote his own. To build an unimpeachable CV, he volunteered everywhere he could — for the homeless, prison inmates, the terminally ill, those with mental health problems — and from these experiences he carefully developed a bank of politically useful anecdotes. By the second year of university, he was already getting opinion pieces published regularly in the broadsheets. A couple of times he'd been quoted in the House. He was becoming a name. He was living entirely for his future, for when the subterfuge of his present would become the substance of his past, his nation's past.

But he did do one thing that was not in his plans. He married Rea, who was a social worker at an office where he did one of his summer placements. Rea, who quickly became pregnant with Megan, loved her job in Birmingham, but for him it was important to be in London. He wanted to do social work for a few years in Camden, which he planned to make his constituency. He convinced Rea of the importance of this move for him, and she agreed, but said that she would only join him when she'd found a job in London equal to the one she had. So he got himself a flat in Camden, and commuted back to Birmingham every weekend.

It was then that he was assigned to Sandra, his first client. She was eighteen. She'd been taken away from her parents at seven years old, having been abused, and from there she'd been in five foster homes and three government-run centers. The list of problems was almost endless: drug and alcohol abuse, shoplifting, three terminated pregnancies, mental health problems involving self-abuse, and a kind of periodic infantile regression. She'd been sexually assaulted and raped a number of times, once by one of her foster fathers.

Sean remembered so vividly the first time she came into

his little office. He noticed, rather guiltily, how tiny her shorts were, and that she was not wearing a bra, her large breasts clearly visible beneath the thin material of her tank top. On her feet were a pair of yellow flipflops. Her toenails had been painted gold. Her face, always partly obscured by her rather badly dyed blonde hair, was soft and dazzled, a truly beautiful face, her lips exactly like the boy's, though her makeup was bright and crude. He could see a few tracks in her arms, and her bare legs, though shapely and still very attractive, were speckled with bruises. She spoke with a childish coquettishness and made sexually provocative gestures that were almost a burlesque, lifting her hair in a great gush above her head to expose her neck, then releasing it, letting it bury her face before hefting it all away again. She played her St. Christopher medallion constantly over her lips and intermittently stretched out her legs to rub and examine them speculatively.

It troubled him to see how helpless she was, quite literally a child inside a woman's body, a very complex, damaged child. He could sense all the compartments in which she lived, as a woman of eighteen, as a child, as a purely sexual being. But this was not all, for when she emptied out her purse to look for her cigarettes, he saw a copy of Gide's *The Immoralist*. When he asked her about the book, her face suddenly became intense, hermetic, as she described a section in it that talked about the birth and death of cultures. She'd then explained how she related such a conception to the people she knew, their own personal cultures, how she always tried to understand the spirit from which those cultures had sprung, and to assess how solid these people had now become. "To be fluid is to be alive," she'd said to him, "and to still have a chance to begin."

Stupidly he'd tried to argue with her at that same level of abstraction in an attempt to keep her being the person who'd said this, as he realized how fragmented a woman she really was, and that there was certainly nothing essentially simple-minded about her — indeed, that it was probably the very acuteness of her sensibility that had made her fragmentation so extreme. But at his challenge, the person who'd said, "To be fluid is to be alive," fell back into her, and just for a moment, looking into her face, he saw between her aspects, saw into the darkness, the chasm, as deep as her sensibility, between her hermetic selves. As her head had sunk, her hair collapsing over her face, he'd placed his hand upon her bare arm.

Sean remembered this now and wondered if perhaps that was the beginning of it, that touch just to steady, to comfort her before she surfaced from her hair, smiling, once more dazzled and diffuse and lovely and empty.

She missed her next three appointments with him. Then one night he went to a pub on the Windsor Estate in Camden, where most of his clients — including Sandra — lived. He'd gone to give legal advice to a group of people in the estate who wanted to form a residents' association to fight for improvements in the council housing. He was there as the unimpeachable politician to come, the man of the people who could speak their language, and among them, subtly, so as not to seem fake, he took on some aspects of Clive, who was one of the twelve children whose lives he'd drawn from his mother's atavistic vision. As Clive, who he'd conceived of as a kind of East End wide-boy, he spoke in the faint cockney of his mother and was, by turns, brash and sentimentally earnest.

After the meeting he had no choice but to drink, pints bought for him, pints he bought for others. He drank also because of the strain of being Clive, of needing to invoke Clive to mediate between him and these people, with whom he felt no real affinity or affection, as if they were a different species.

Finally, he couldn't bear it any longer, and was about to leave when Sandra walked into the pub. On seeing Sean, she made straight for him with a sure smile as if she'd intended to meet him here. She ignored all the men who called suggestively to her and ordered a drink, which Sean paid for. She wore a pair of six-inch stilettos, a tiny skirt, and a halter top, her lips wet with lipstick. He tried not to look at her body, tried not to be affected by her crude flirtation, kept reminding himself that she was ill. At one stage she went to the bathroom, and he willed himself to leave, but could not. He'd never felt this kind of compulsion — or rather this kind of helplessness — and didn't know where it had come from.

Still, eighteen years on, as Sean stared out at the lonely silhouette of a crane huddled beneath the railway bridge, he could hardly believe it. He'd just got married to a woman he loved madly, a woman, moreover, who'd just given birth to his child, and who trusted him. But he did know that he hadn't been attracted just to the sex that Sandra had wielded so crudely. Though undoubtedly at a different level of beauty than most, in her sexuality Sandra was a very familiar type to him. Roy, one of his colleagues in the office, called them beeps — buxom East End peroxides — flowering early and fading quickly into the barest, the most seedy and tattered lineaments of desire. And Sean was a handsome and charismatic man who'd met, since he'd married Rea, a great number of lovely and available women without ever once having felt the slightest temptation to stray.

Sandra had returned from the bathroom in a fog of perfume, all her makeup reapplied. He'd said he'd see her home, but she'd told him that there was someone staying at her flat and she didn't want to go back there. So he drove her to his flat, trying to believe in his own drunkenness, though some essential part of him remained absolutely sober, telling him that she was ill, that this was wrong.

In the hallway, she'd almost fallen. He'd taken hold of her. They'd clung together, she was laughing, her head upon his shoulder. Then she'd lifted her head, her hair pouring away from it, her face exposed. That lovely mouth, the boy's mouth, panted alcohol at him. It was then that he'd kissed her; it was then that it had been too late.

Sean, again hearing those girls out on the deck laughing, fisted his hands upon the filthy kitchen counter. Once more — for the thousandth, for the hundred-thousandth time in his life — he tried to understand why he'd done it. God, if he could unweave one black thread from his life, knotted there at that place; if he could just unravel her mouth and her face and her body; if he could take back that kiss. Where had it come from, that sabotage of a life he was trying to make substantial, remembered? Perhaps it was Clive who'd kissed her, perhaps one cannot invoke a life, even an imagined life, even in jest or idleness, without accepting the risk of being unbalanced by some sudden eddy of that life's fate.

Afterward, Sandra had pulled herself out of the bed beside him and he'd heard her vomiting in the bathroom. He remembered the image of her returning to his bed, the bathroom light behind her making her face a black void in the ragged cowl of her hair. Getting in beside him, she'd curled up fetally and had begun to sing incoherently to herself; and he kept thinking, "Christ, what have I done?"

For Sean, that was the end of all his ambitions, his sense of future. On the most practical level, he'd just done something that could destroy any career he might attempt to build — indeed, if it was discovered he would have lost his job, his wife, everything he cared about. But deeper than that, his plan had required him to be perfect, unimpeachable; and this one aberration had now broken the tension of it all. He'd taken advantage, in full knowledge, as her caseworker, of a woman who'd been sexually abused all her life, a woman with severe mental health problems, a woman as vulnerable as could be conceived. And yet . . . and yet hadn't a part of him felt a kind of relief in this ruination; wasn't this his real face, the face of his father as they'd lifted him from the pavement, his lips smeared with wine and blood, a face he'd denied? It was the relief of

dimension. *This* was not subterfuge. *This,* in full consciousness, was the now at the expense of all future. He placed his
hand gently upon her huddled form. She was real. This had
happened.

But then the terror, the shame had welled up again, the
thought of losing his wife, his job, all of his ambitions. For
a second, looking down at the side of Sandra's lovely face,
her eyes quivering with dreams, he'd wanted to kill her.
And not just to kill her, but to eradicate her, to crush her
into a ball, to crush that ball into an atom, to burst that
atom between his fingernails like a tick. Yes, he wanted to
kill her. Not that he could ever do such a thing, but he
arrived vividly at that point where he could understand a
person who could do such a thing. And, in as much as he
still thought of himself as a good man, he could understand
that a person may kill — even under the most sordid circumstances — may kill and not be evil, may kill and still
even be good.

But that was not the worst.

Perhaps if it had ended there with that one night something might have been recouped, but he'd continued to see
her, or rather, periodically, she'd continued to turn up at his
flat. She was his hopelessness, his terror, his end as much as
Rea had been his life. And he'd never turned her away. She
was the face of his father, rogue in the world, a face he
should have kissed in front of them all, the wedding party,
and should have said, This is my father. He has struck the
earth.

And none of this, nothing, nothing but weakness, the

desire of subterfuge for substance, even the easy substance of ruination. Perhaps not even that, just the desire for chaos, to couple with the incommensurable. Yes.

Yes, she kept turning up at his door. Their sexual life continued. Sometimes she was drunk or drugged. Once, she was crying, her cheek bruised, her dress ripped at the strap. Often men dropped her off, men driving old Cortinas and Capris. At weekends he commuted back to his home in Birmingham, lied to his wife. In London he lived in constant fear, never invited anyone to his flat because he never knew when she was going to turn up. He began to worry about disease, from the needles she used, from the other men. And then she told him that she'd missed her period.

He begged her to get an abortion. They fought, and he was amazed by how shocked and hurt she was. Despite the other men, she obviously considered him a kind of husband, his flat as their home, these sexual interludes as their married life. Finally, she stormed out.

This terrified him. She could destroy his life. He kept expecting her to come into the office and make a scene. But a month went by without any sign of her. Quickly he took a job in Birmingham, telling his boss he had marital problems, telling his wife he missed her and the baby too much — which was true, because he'd felt the possible loss of them so vividly. He knew his wife well enough to know that her love for him, made precarious by its very intensity, would not survive one indiscretion, let alone such an infidelity, and it made him sick to think of the kind of pain that this was waiting to unleash upon Rea, who was now pregnant with Liam.

At home he was always terrified of that knock that might come at the door. And it was just a few weeks before the birth of his son that he found out from Roy, his old colleague in the Camden office, that "that crazy beep" had had a child, a boy.

So the fear intensified. He felt that any day she might turn up at his door with the child. But at the same time he himself had developed a kind of morbid fascination with her and the boy, the kind of fascination one might have for a wound that one senses is mortal. One knows and yet one does not believe — he thought now of those powerful, evil men, incredulous of their own deaths, in his daughter's diary.

He kept in touch with Roy and worked Sandra into every conversation. This was not difficult, for Roy's only way of surviving emotionally after twenty years as a social worker was to have contempt for all his clients.

Yes, Roy loved to talk about that crazy beep with the big tits, God, if she was his client he'd give her some therapy. Roy would say these hateful things to relieve the vast lie of his life, which in its way, its routine and in its true effect on those around him, was as abstemious and virtuous as a monk's. He turned up to his job every day, every night went to the Duke with his colleagues, drank six pints and steeped himself in the toxic effluence of their gossip. Then two dutiful pints of water before falling into his single bed, the sheets of which he hadn't changed in four months, and finally he would draw up through his nostrils, from the scent of his own dried sweat, dreams of all the Sandras.

But they were only dreams, and he could not hear the

quickened beat of Sean's heart as he told Sean that the kid was called, of all things, Tobias, that they'd taken him away from her three times now. But then she'd turn up in hot pants to that pillock, Alvin, and convince him she was well enough to look after the boy again. If he'd let her speak, Roy said, if he didn't have other uses for that lovely mouth of hers.

Every week Sean endured Roy's hateful, self-loathing, and impotent puerility because, despite the chances that the father could be any number of men, Sean felt somehow sure that the boy was his. And his interest in this boy increased as his hopes for his own children decreased. Having failed at his perfect life, he'd tried so hard to end the cycle of ruination with himself, to have Megan and Liam understand how short and fragile, how completely precarious life is. But perhaps he'd taught it to them while they were too young, for they'd learned it too well, learned it in their bodies. They had developed more and more problems, his son so sick, his daughter clinically depressed. Then Rea had an ectopic pregnancy, after which she'd been given a hysterectomy. Following this, his fascination with the boy had become more extreme, and one time he'd even returned to the Windsor housing estate, had waited for hours early in the morning outside Sandra's flat until he'd seen her and the boy coming out. The boy was about seven, but was holding her hand as if she were the child, speaking to her calmly and with a paternal frown. He was a beautiful boy, his shame and his son. His son.

Then it happened.

By chance, it was one of his wife's special days, selected spontaneously that morning as she'd looked out at the pouring rain, and selected, he knew, because of that profound unhappiness she could sense in him. She'd made him call in sick to work and had excused the kids from school. They watched videos, played games, and then everyone helped in the preparation of the most elaborate four-course dinner. But just before they sat down to that dinner, Roy had phoned. He asked Sean if he'd heard what had happened. Roy was excited, pleased with his news, being coy. Finally he said it: the beep with the big tits. Dead. Murdered. She'd been found in a derelict brewery by the Thames, beaten and strangled, her naked body covered in a piece of blue tarpaulin. The boy had been taken into a home.

After putting the phone down, Sean had walked into the bathroom, locking himself in. He'd sat down on the edge of the bath, had sunk his head into his hands, and had cried for joy, that wonderful, painful relief like a not quite healed scab eased from the rawness of his soul. He'd cried and then, crying and laughing still, he'd paced about the tiny bathroom, wanting to break everything — not in anger, but from the pure excess of his joy, all his nerves blossoming. Finally as his wife had knocked on the door for him, he'd tried to bring himself back to earth, to feel some grief, had forced himself to imagine what exactly had happened to her, to Sandra — her name was Sandra — of that night, her beating, her corpse. But he could not subdue his euphoria.

It was as if all his senses had suddenly returned to him. At that special dinner no food had ever tasted more delicious. He'd never felt more love for his wife and his children, as if they'd come back from the dead. He could not stop touching them.

That night, he and his wife had made love with all the passion of their first nights together. And as she'd been looking into his eyes, as she'd said that this was one of the happiest days of her life, it was then that the grief had finally come, the grief and the self-loathing, because this woman whom he loved so deeply was responding to the happiness in him generated by the most profound iniquity. Rea would place this day, their intimacy, among all those other treasures she'd rescued from time. She'd taken photographs of him smiling at dinner, kissing his children, kissing her, and beneath them, beneath each smile and kiss, as beneath that piece of blue tarpaulin in the basement of a derelict brewery, lay Sandra's corpse. He imagined those photographs in his wife's albums turning black, curling, bursting spontaneously into flame, destroying everything. And inside his wife he imagined that hidden mendacity, like a worm, slowly corrupting all her memories.

It all came down on him so hard, that torrent of loathing and guilt. It made him physically ill. A sore developed in his eye that would not go away. He started out of sleep at night with panic attacks. For a short while he even began to believe that *he* had killed Sandra. Indeed was there not some responsibility for what had happened to her in the desire he'd felt that first time he'd taken her back to his flat to kill her, that understanding, at least, of the desire to kill?

And the truth was that that desire, that understanding, had remained alive through all these years until those hands had finally closed about her throat.

He became, for a while, obsessed with the murder itself. He found out every detail he could, and a year to the day after it had happened he'd actually broken into that derelict brewery by the river and had remained all night in the place where her body had been found.

He'd then sought out the boy, who'd been fostered a couple of times, but had always been returned prematurely to government-run centers. One set of foster parents claimed that the boy, at just nine years old, had broken up their marriage, though no more details were given. In another foster home, the parents had said that his "street maturity" was a disruptive influence on their natural children. It was added by the social worker that the boy's intelligence and verbal capacity were causing problems in the family, especially with the self-esteem of one of their natural sons, who was close to the boy's age. Here was something Sean felt he might be able to recoup, draw out unsullied from the mire of his life. So, after convincing Rea, who'd wanted more children anyway, that it was better to foster before making a decision to adopt, and after a little bit of wrangling with an old college friend of his who, by chance, managed the home in which the boy was living, he fostered Tobias, Pierce, the boy.

Sean inhaled the rotting damp of the boat, in which he was sealed, as by a shell of the thinnest glass, by the laughter of those girls on deck, those children, wasting time. If only he could have that time they did not need. And these thoughts, like all his thoughts and memories since he'd stepped into the cabin, he realized now, were a circuitous route to just one impulse.

He went down the creaking stairway, entered that dank corridor of cabins filled with muffled voices and the smell of marijuana, and knocked on Caitlín's door.

12

FROM INSIDE THE CABIN, her voice sang out, "Come in."

She was sitting at a desk she'd made by resting a piece of wood over the sink. She'd obviously been studying, her books piled around her, but was now dabbing a clear liquid onto the tips of her nails.

"It's meant to stop you biting them, this stuff, but I've acquired the taste now, so I put it on just before I bite them." She smiled and suddenly remembered — "Did you find him?" she asked, turning her chair around and using her bare foot to push a pile of clothes off an armchair that took up half the cabin.

"No," he said, as he sat down. "And I've been picking up boys outside Victoria Station all night."

She gave him a camp, suggestive look, which he met with a watery smile, adding, "Only one of them really helped me. I have to look for a fat man in a gray van in Tower Hamlets."

She laughed; he too began to laugh.

"A fat man in a gray van in Tower Hamlets," she repeated melodiously. "Sounds like a line from one of those dreadful 'poems on the underground.'"

"And the worst thing," he went on, "is that I'm now definitely on the metropolitan police's pedophile list."

"Well, it's good to belong."

Still smiling, they looked into each other's eyes for a few moments, just too long, until hers flickered safely away.

"Would you like some wine?" she asked, standing, suddenly nervous. "I have some in the fridge upstairs. If it's not been nicked."

"Sure," he said and she slipped out into the corridor.

Like his own, her cabin was a six-foot box containing a bunk bed, a sink, and a porthole. Into this she'd imported the armchair on which he sat, a desk chair, a squat chest of drawers painted lilac, and a framed picture of *The Kiss,* by Klimt. He looked around at her clothes on the floor, her scattered cosmetics, her textbooks upon that makeshift desk. It all cocooned her; she was waiting for a new life. And yet it seemed so precarious, and despite himself he felt a shade of pity — not for her, but for himself, for feeling for something so fragile. She was so much like his wife, a tiny spider whose web could dissolve at a single breath, just to be woven with undiminished fervor and hope somewhere else. It was an indomitable fragility, while his apparent invulnerability had been something that could be only irretrievably destroyed, a shattered idol — in the dark mouth, the carved eye, the hollow ear of which, the tiny spiders would begin to weave their webs. But this room, this frail web, had, in raising the ghost of his wife, raised a question: did he have a chance still for a normal life? Could he forget the boy and what the boy had done?

No. Even the impulse which had brought him to her room was hopeless. Even as he felt his attraction for her, wanted her — or wanted his desire for her — he couldn't escape the knowledge that there was nothing solid beneath him. For a moment Sean's head reeled. Vertigo. A narrow ledge, miles high. But then he heard her descend the stairs, and as he steadied himself, inhaling the perfume of her room, as he thought of his wife, her tenderness, their intimacy, her body, some ghost of hope arose that he might yet grope his way back past the memory of loss into some semblance of life. And as she entered, thrusting toward him the bottle and the opener, this woman, vivid and demanding, all the possibilities of the wine and this small room set off a wave of exhilaration in him that was almost fear. He'd not touched, nor thought of touching, a woman in three years.

After dismantling her desk, she washed out a couple of mugs and filled them with wine. As they sipped, a tense silence reigned. Sean felt that she knew what he'd been feeling, and found it difficult to look into her eyes. Both of them were so out of place in this boat reeking of languorous youth, the time all around them going to waste, in the strumming of the guitar, in the plaiting of the hair, in the heady, melancholic fog of weed.

Finally she leaned in toward him, frowning like a child,

and demanded in a tone of mock interrogation, "So come on now, who are you?"

Looking directly at her, he smiled. "You're so Irish," he said.

"All right, well, what do you *do*? Let's just begin with that."

"I'm a social worker. I manage an office in Solihull."

"Well, that's one thing we have in common — or will have in common when — *if* — I become a social worker. And the divorce, that's two." At this, her eyes once again flickered away.

"When did you get divorced?" he asked.

"It was official just over a year ago now."

"And was it . . . clean?"

"What a way of putting it. Unfortunately no. As mild-mannered as he seemed, he threatened everything from killing himself to killing me. One time he hid under my car and took hold of my ankle as I was about to get in. I think the whole thing was completely impulsive on his part. He was in his suit. The idea must have just struck him as he was on his way to work."

"So what happened?"

"Well, it was actually quite funny in a sad sort of way. I managed to pull myself free, but he got hold of my shoe, and by this time there was a whole crowd of people who'd heard me scream gathered around the car, all of us peering beneath it at this pure incarnation of actuarial accountancy in his three-piece suit clutching at my plimsoll and weeping like a child." She frowned a little. "I know I must sound cold to you, but truthfully I couldn't really feel anything for him. I'd stayed with him two years longer than I should have just because I didn't want to hurt his feelings. I just wanted him out of my life. I wanted *to have* some kind of life. I'd always gone out with whatever men asked me to, amazed and grateful — God, you couldn't even imagine some of the horrors I dragged back to mother. To them I was always sweet, incompetent Caitlín; and I hated it really, hated myself, spent so many days eating pounds of chocolate-coated marshmallows, watching *Pebble Mill,* wallowing in self-loathing."

"So you've not had any relationships since — "

"Wait a minute. You accused *me* of being Irish. What about you?"

"What about me?"

"Well, since we're on the subject of divorces . . . ?"

Sean sipped the wine. After a moment, he said, "She left me about three years ago." He took another sip, making a slight moue, as if the wine had gone sour, and went on quietly, "We had some terrible things happen. We lost both our children. We had a boy and a girl. The boy, Liam, had some medical problems — a chronic asthmatic condition — so his death was not entirely a shock to us, and I suppose, in a way, neither was Megan's. She suffered from clinical depression — very profound — chemical apparently, some imbalance. She killed herself."

"I'm so sorry," Caitlín said softly, hunched over, both hands wrapped around her mug of wine.

"So . . . things were difficult," he said.

"Was Devon with you then?"

"Yes, he was. And that was the reason — part of the reason — we had to give him up."

"Did he understand?"

"Well, he was young."

"So that's why you're looking for him — to explain?"

"Yes . . ." Sean, staring blankly into his drink, repeated mechanically, "to explain."

All the fury, the pain, again had descended. He was sitting with a mug of cheap wine in a tiny cabin with a woman he didn't know and through whom he wanted to find a way back into his life. He observed how she differed from his wife — her dark hair, her long feet, her large, round, naked eyes. But he just couldn't take hold of these features, as if his senses were no longer fluid enough to simulate them, to place their image in the soul, which is love. Was it too late? Had his sense already established its idols, its forms? Was it too late to take, as a metaphor for feeling, that long brown hair, draped over one side of this woman's lovely face, those long feet, those wide, porous eyes?

"Would you like some more wine?" she said, raising the bottle toward him.

"Not tonight," he said, covering the mouth of his cup and standing. "I should get some sleep."

She stood also, taking his cup and putting it in the sink. In the tiny cabin, they were close.

"You're tall," he said.

"I've always hated being tall."

"No, it's nice."

She smiled, as at something secret.

"Can I take you to dinner tomorrow night?" he found himself saying.

She seemed to consider this for a moment, to inwardly sigh and swallow some small scruple.

"All right," she said.

13

LIAM HAS JUST GOT BACK from the hospital after another terrible attack. He almost died this time, but Durward says it doesn't matter. Whatever doesn't kill us makes us stronger. He tells Liam about this philosopher called Nietzsche (Neecha). He talks of the Superman and tells Liam that no matter how weak he feels he must strive to live. To strive, to seek, to find, and not to yield. He reads him poetry and adventure stories by Conrad and Jack London. We've moved his bed so Liam now looks toward his window, toward life. I've said sometimes to Durward that I'm worried, because Liam is so weak, but Durward still insists on taking him outside with us whenever he gets the chance. He tells me, and it thrills me, the way he says it (he's having me read Camus, Sartre, and Céline, as well as Cocteau) — he says that like the twins in *Les Enfants Terribles* he and I inhabit our own world, that there is nowhere for us but death. But a death met upon our own terms, met in the fullness of life, not when we're old, with failing bodies, and have no choice, no will. That we will never collapse in front of strangers, twitching and incontinent. That we must die while we are still more spirit than meat. And he says that Liam may go first, as our child, to be reborn. Yes, he is like our child and I can see how much he loves Durward. Durward tells him that he must move from strength to strength, that by sheer will he shall become the Superman, that the body is nothing. He gets him out of bed sometimes, and that's when I become a little scared, when I see my brother's wracked and skinny body, when I see that his will is his pure love for Durward, for —————. Sometimes Liam falls into a coughing fit, and we help him back to bed, and between us we hold him until he can find his breath. Then Durward looks across at me, over my brother's head, and there is no lie in his eyes — a hive without a queen. I know my brother must die, and we too.

Liam went to the hospital this time because we took him outside, took him to the lake. We should have been at school, but Durward can get us off school at any time. He can forge Dad's writing perfectly, and also does a flawless imitation of Dad's voice on the phone. It's eerie to watch him being Dad, to see his transformation, how he sits and gestures like Dad and uses all his particular phrases. I think it was the cold water that caused Liam to collapse. We carried him back. I was sure he was going to die. We told Mum and Dad that he'd just had an attack in his room. The hospital wanted to keep him, but Liam was miserable without us both, and Durward managed to convince Mum, as he always can, to bring Liam home.

14

RONAN BURST INTO THE DOOR of the boys' home, breathing heavily. He threw his shopping down by the telephone seat and ran up the stairs and into his mother's room. She sat almost insensible in the chair, her face frozen but for a slight twitch at the turn of her lip.

"Damn you," he screamed.

Quickly he prepared the insulin, injected it into her, and then sat on her bed clutching his head between his hands as she came round.

"I forgot again," she said, her face still too sluggish to form any definite expression. Though eighty-three years old, no one could doubt that she was Ronan's mother, the same deep-set and heavy-browed eyes, the same beakish mouth.

Finally, completely refocused, she switched on the television with her remote control, turning off the sound and staring at it with the same baffled, wide-eyed attention a baby has for some passing stimulus. After a moment, she glanced back over at her son, who still held his head in his hands.

"Oh, come on," she said, "you've always had a tendency to dramatics. It's so effeminate. Brion never made a fuss about anything. Even when he broke his arm — "

"Brion?" he shouted, cutting her off, looking up. "Brion's an alcoholic. Brion's living on social security and moonlighting on building sites at fifty years old. Brion has not come to visit you once in ten years. If you were living with Brion you'd be dead right now — a hundred times dead."

At this she withdrew from him completely, staring into the television, her lips stubbornly pursed.

"I can't be here every day to make sure you're taking your medicine," he continued uselessly shouting. "I have this home to run. I have a life. I have *my* life. I've tried to get you nurses."

"I can't have these nurses," she spat out archly. "That last one reeked and she was as common as muck. I told her she stank and should go back to her brood of kids. She had an abortion, you know, when she was fifteen — *fifteen*. I told her she'd murdered that child and condemned it to Hell because it hadn't been baptized. I told her that such a sin would curse all her children in the end — Ezra chapter eleven, verse three: 'And her fruit grew whole without, but tasted as ashes on the tongue.'"

"That's a lie! There's no such verse."

His mother snatched up the remote control. Both of them now wore exactly the same face, their lips pursed, their eyes brooding and brutal.

Flipping furiously, senselessly through the silent channels, she continued. "And that other one was black. I'm sure she was stealing my syringes and I caught her once putting her finger in my soup to see if it was too hot. Her filthy finger! That same finger she used to lick when she was reading that book of hers. 'And the Lord cast them out as abominations; they were brothers to dragons, their skin was black upon them; and their bones were burned with heat.' And as for me, 'My harp is turned to mourning and my organ into the voice of them that weep.'"

Ronan groaned, sinking his face back into his hands. His mother had a particular method with the nurses. For about a week she'd be sweet and inquisitive, getting them to reveal all kinds of confidences. And after she'd garnered enough information she would begin to use these confidences against the nurses in the most vicious and relentless manner.

He looked up at her. He could see the flickering of the television's images in her vacant eyes, as if they were the flames of a fire. How much longer would she live, he wondered, but then felt immediately guilty. Recently he'd begun to think about this quite often, to feel, with a kind of terror, that he would be an old man before she was gone. Could he stand ten, twenty years more of this? He couldn't even leave the house for half a day. Either she wouldn't take her insulin or she'd inject too much of it. He'd tried to convince her to go into a home, but she'd refused, and he hadn't been able to bring himself to insist. All the homes he'd speculatively visited had been so depressing, filled with dazzled old people, like little chess pieces from sets long broken up and lost, propped in chairs and listing into a dead sleep, or with just enough energy to make birdlike their opaque eyes; and the ancient women, their knee-stockings falling down around their ankles, singing old songs in voices as brittle as their bones, and dancing waltzes, spinning as slowly as the fragments of shattered planets in space. God, but she made his life Hell, she did, but hadn't she suffered to bring him and his brother up, a woman who'd taken tea with the prime minister of Ireland, the ambassador of Brazil, struggling after a disastrous marriage which took her from her father's large estate in Mayo to a council estate in Swiss Cottage, struggling always to bring them up good boys. And he had been a good boy, had done well in school, had never been in trouble, had helped her constantly, had felt at times that he'd grafted his nerves to hers, felt nothing of his own. In return all her emotional energy went into Brion, as Brion slipped out of her home and into the pubs and bookies. For all the heartache he caused her, it was Brion she'd loved the most — handsome, funny, and ruined, just as her husband had been. When he infrequently returned, she became like an infatuated teenager. It was as if life had returned, though Ronan could see that her love frightened, saddened, and ultimately revolted Brion. So after eating, after finally accepting the money she kept thrusting into his pockets, Brion would disappear again, leaving her evacuated and irritable. And not once had his mother ever shown any real love for Ronan, not once had she ever congratulated him for passing his exams, for winning every school prize, for helping her in the home, not once had she ever laughed at his fledgling humor, not once in front of him had she ever become innocent and susceptible to suffering. And not once had she ever supported him, even after the incident with the woman at his parish, which had thrust him from the church and from his life.

She continued to gaze into the flickering television.

"I'll bring your milk and digestives in an hour," he said, getting up.

"I only eat McVitie's. Those digestives that girl got — they were not McVitie's."

"I'll go and buy you some now," he said, and waited for just a moment to see if she would thank him. She said nothing.

He put on his coat and went downstairs. After checking himself in the hall mirror, he turned to go and saw, in the letter cage, a letter, hand delivered and addressed to him. He recognized the writing — not the form of it, for the style was always slightly different, but the soul of it. Instantly he snatched it out. As soon as he'd read it, he checked his watch and left the house as frantically as he'd entered it.

15

THE BUS into Tower Hamlets seemed to take forever. Following the instructions in the letter, Ronan sat on a bench by the towpath in front of Corbet's Glassworks. The evening grayness was like a fog, Tower Bridge just visible in the distance. He felt panicked. He'd promised his mother he would be back in an hour. She'd raise a terrible fuss if she didn't get her warm milk and biscuits. Theresa would bring it to her, but she hated Theresa, and Theresa hated her. His mother would be insufferable for days. And in two and a half hours, she needed another injection. But these thoughts were just an annoying buzz in his mind, like that of an insect when one is trying to sleep. He checked his watch. She was late. A young woman strolled by, walking her dog, and he felt an anticipatory welling of lust in the pit of his stomach, a feeling at once irresistible and sickening. An hour went by. Still he waited. Two hours. He had to go. His mother would not take her medicine. The panic began to swell in his chest, but that black longing kept him where he was, enervating him. Finally he heard the crunch of her shoes on the towpath. She sat down at the end of his bench. Pushing her thick red curls back over her shoulders, she glanced at him modestly, and gave him a brief, nervous smile. She crossed her lovely legs, tugging a little at the hem of her short skirt, and let her scuffed red shoe unhinge from her foot. Finally, she pulled a book from her shopping bag and began to read.

"*The Longest Journey,*" Ronan said, referring to her book. "How are you liking it?"

"It's good so far," she said, glancing at him shyly.

"You know, I once sat in that same room in Cambridge where he talks about seeing those cows right at the beginning."

"Really," she said with admiration, glancing at him more directly now. Nervously, she uncrossed and recrossed her legs. Her skirt rode up and she tugged it back down, blushing.

"Yes. I have to say I find that particular work a little jejune, but *A Passage to India* has to be one of the best novels written this century."

"You sound as if you read a great deal."

"I used to." And as if in explanation: "I was a Jesuit at one stage."

She looked confused.

"It means that I was a little gnostic fart in a habit. I had faith in knowing. With the passion of youth I shook myself up until the oil of the soul, the water of the flesh, and the air of the mind seemed almost like one substance, indivisible as the Trinity."

Still she was baffled, becoming obviously embarrassed.

He stripped the sarcasm from his tone. "It's a Catholic order — known for their rather scholarly bias. Have you ever read *The Portrait of an Artist* by Joyce?"

She shook her head. "I think he's probably too difficult for me at the moment," she said quietly.

"Oh, I'm sure not," he instantly rejoined with vehemence and tenderness. "I'm sure not."

"I've really just started with my reading," she said, as if apologizing. "My husband's a long-distance lorry driver and he's not much for books. In fact he won't really allow me to have books in the house. Says they'll put ideas in my head."

"Oh, that's terrible. Do you have to hide them?"

"Well, I just put them in the dresser with my underwear. He'd never go in there. But the librarian's always remarking how the books I bring back smell of lavender."

Her coy smile turned slightly impish, and she impulsively lifted her book to his face.

He sniffed at the book and laughed. "It does," he said.

As if frightened of their sudden intimacy, her eyes withdrew from his as she placed the book back upon her lap, rubbing its cover nervously with her fingers as the silence between them expanded.

"Do you live near here?" Ronan said finally.

"I do," she said, adding after a modest pause, "Would you like a cup of tea or something?"

"I'd love one."

As they walked they exchanged names — hers was Hilary. She questioned him about what books he thought she should read, and he suggested *Justine,* quoting two long passages. She had such a lovely face, a sweet laugh, and the nervous habit of lifting her hair into her mouth. Finally, she led him down into a basement studio. It was sweltering and humid, four heaters working at full blast. From behind the back door, he could hear a dog whining.

Hilary took his coat and threw it, together with her own, over the back of an armchair. Sweat was already beginning to bead on Ronan's forehead. She turned on a small lamp in the corner of the room, then walked right past him to switch off the main light. He could smell the scent of lavender in the room. His head ached with it.

She now came right up close to him.

"My husband won't be back until five-thirty," she said, pinching her own fingers and glancing up at him nervously. His desire for her as well as the heat in the room was sapping. His breath came shallowly and he felt light-headed as he looked down at those lovely, sculpted lips. He put his hands upon her shoulders, holding them softly, tremulously at first, but then more forcefully, causing her to buckle a little, to let out a small cry as Ronan sank to his knees, dragging his hands almost brutally down the length of her body, pressing his head finally into her belly.

Placing her hands upon his cheeks, she eased him up again, kissed him and led him to the bed. He lay on top of her, breathing her, running his hands like an adolescent over her body, tugging at her clothes but not removing them as she began to make small moans, the heat drenching them both in sweat.

Suddenly he pulled himself away.

"I have to go," he said. "I have to go."

She lay impassively for a moment as he looked down at her, then reached for him. He kissed her face, her neck, ran his hand beneath her blouse. She began to undo his shirt, and every now and then pressed gently into his groin with her hand.

"Christ, Christ," he said, finally pulling himself away. "I've got to go. I've got to go. My mother — "

She bit gently at his ear, her warm breath, her perfume. He wanted so much to succumb, tried to imagine her desolate, lonely life, to imagine her husband's rough body upon hers, all her longings. Her life was almost real and he was almost lost; but once more it broke in, the face of his mother this morning, empty, that muscle in her mouth twitching like the leg of a crushed insect. He pulled himself up from the bed, doing up his buttons, looking down at that prone woman, who stared at him now almost coldly.

"One more chance," she said, "and then it's all gone."

Ronan tried to touch her face, but she turned away.

16

THE BOY PULLED OFF HIS WIG, removed the skirt and blouse, wiped off all his makeup, and lay naked again upon the damp bed. The dog still whined behind the door. Alex watched the sluggish clock in the heat. For three hours, unmoved, he watched it, watched each minute pass. At five-thirty it chimed, and the alarms of all the other clocks went off. Less than a minute later came the sound of the fatman pounding down the stairs, fumbling with his keys, dropping them, and finally getting the door open. He charged into the room and switched off all the alarms that were still ringing. For a moment the fatman couldn't speak, leaning back against the wall, his eyes tight shut, his face crimson, his whole body heaving for breath. The naked boy in the heat watched him impassively.

"It's . . . it's . . . too 'ard," the fatman forced out between snatched breaths. "It's too 'ard for me to get 'ome in 'alf an 'our . . . The . . . the traffic. And the buses, they're full . . . sometimes." He slid down to the floor, breathing through clenched teeth. The boy smiled. The fatman's fly was gaping open.

Hearing his master's voice, the dog began to howl, scratching frantically at the back door. The fatman cast a guilty, stricken look over at the shut door but said nothing.

The fatman now wore a watch on each wrist, as well as a nurse's timepiece hanging over his shirt pocket. The boy had bought him all of these from various pawn shops. Alex loved the pawn shops. Perhaps because nothing was new, so each object had its fate. Maybe this is what he occupied himself with as he lay for hours on the bed — imagining what would cause a nurse to give up so vital a piece of her equipment, conjuring whole lives, bringing them to the points of desperation that would lead to the selling of these objects, which thus became burdened with some hopelessness. And even if they'd simply been found or stolen, all of them had been worn *into* other lives and thus carried with them the vagrant eddies of other fates. If you wear a pair of shoes worn by another man, you condemn yourself to admix with your own gait something of his roll and pitch, and because people are as much — perhaps more — surface and gesture as they are depth and soul, because people are made as much from the outside in as the inside out, so they add some tone and tincture of that man's fate to their own. And this, the boy perhaps intuited, was why the fatman could never be on time — because no matter how fastidiously synchronized they were, these watches had different times. The time of the nurse's watch, beating softly against her breast as she ran from ward to ward; the time of that elegant watch with the gold face, which belonged to a man of taste and leisure, a lady's man who, on principle, was always late; the time of that heavy steel watch which, despite showing the time in three different places in the world, had once been on the wrist of an illiterate chef who'd never left London, but used the watch to excuse his chronic drinking — "Yes, I know it's only ten in the morning *here,* but in Singapore it's opening time. Cheers."

"I'm sorry," the fatman said, checking one of his watches, "I can't stay up late no more. We been up past three in the mornin' every night. And I find it so 'ard to sleep when you read me them 'orror stories. I was late to work. I got to get some sleep. Vinny said 'e'd fire me if I was late again."

"Well, you won't be late again," the boy said. "I'm going to leave."

The fatman opened his eyes. "No," he cried out, "No, no, no, no, no, *no, no.*" He crawled over to the bed, pathetic terror in his face, down which sweat peeled. "I only worry 'cause I wouldn't be able to get no money to buy you your favorites."

Gently Alex touched the fatman's cheek, but the boy's face was implacable.

"No, no," the fatman called out, resting both his hands in supplication upon the boy's stomach. "There's nothin' else for me. I think about you all the time, every minute, and I don't mind being tired. I like it. I do. I like it. It's like I'm in a dream when I'm working. I can 'ear your voice. I can feel you like you're there. And I loved it last night, staying up with you. I love the way you make all those things up, make us become all those other people in other places. You're my life," he said, softly, desperately. "I couldn't live without you. Not now. Not now."

"Yes, you could. You could just pick up the boys in Victoria like you used to."

"No, no. They're not like you. There's no one like you. And you sing to me. I love it when you sing to me. At work I 'ear you sing to me; and that's why I don't mind being tired in the day. I don't mind my days being dreams because my nights . . . that's when I live. And you're everywhere in my dreams too; and all those different people and places you make up, they're more real than all the people I know. And the other day I 'eard your voice singing to me on the radio, and I felt you breathing on my neck. I felt it. And I was fast asleep, would you believe it, in one of them toilet cubicles, kneeling there with my 'ead on the seat."

The boy's face had softened, conceded something, and he began pushing his hand thoughtfully through the fatman's hair. The dog, which had been whining and scratching all this time, let out a series of desperate yelps as if it were being kicked. Feeling that the boy had now forgiven him, the fatman glanced toward the back door and timidly said, "'Ave you fed Feederboy?"

"Of course I've fed him," the boy said.

"'E likes cump'ny, Feederboy."

"If I'm going to stay," the boy said, "you've got to get rid of the dog."

The fatman looked frightened. His hands were rubbing very gently over the boy's stomach.

"Me and Feederboy been together a long time."

"What are you saying?"

"No, I just mean, 'e's a good dog. We're friends, mates."

"I just can't have him here anymore. He disturbs me. He messes everything up. He's always whining, always wanting something. I can't stand it the way he looks at me, as if I'm cruel. He resents me."

"'E's just a dog."

"Well, you're just a dog too — and so am I." Alex now leaned his face in close to the fatman's, visibly inhaled that confluence of odors — the smell of sweat, ammonia, the changing rooms, the toilets, and of fear and longing. "Our souls are in our noses," he said, just touching his soft cheek to the fatman's coarse bristles and very gently biting the fatman's ear.

"But 'e's too old. No one would 'ave 'im and 'e wouldn't 'ave no one else. Not now. 'E's old. They don't last long that breed and I won't get another one. If I took him down the dog's 'ome they only keep 'em for a few months 'fore they put 'em down and I couldn't put 'im back in the cages, I couldn't do it, not after all this time. 'E's my mate, bin with me twelve years." The dog whined piteously. "Twelve years 'e's bin with me. I couldn't take 'im back to the dog's 'ome. I got 'im from there, I couldn't take 'im back."

"You're not going to take him back. If I hated that dog more than anything in the world — and I don't — but even if I did, I wouldn't have you take him back. Because he's like us, his soul is in his nose, and if you take him back it means his life never happened, which means that a part of you never happened. You can't pull your memories out like a loose thread from a sweater. If he was my most bitter enemy, I would never have you do that to him. He's *yours*, *your* responsibility. It's for you to tie him off, to end him." There was such a vehemence in the boy's voice, right at the fatman's ear, where his face still was.

"But 'e's innocent." The fatman was crying now. "'E's not done nothing." And if the fatman could have seen the boy's face, pressed beside his own, he would have seen that it was red, wild, pressured. The fatman tried to pull away, to look into the boy's eyes, but the boy quickly took hold of his head, held him in until he'd controlled himself, until the return of his stone face, which he finally revealed to the fatman.

"Yes, he's innocent," Alex said. "Not like people, not like children. No human is innocent. You know, they like you at Victoria," the boy said with a sudden change of tone, "because you always pay them, you're never rough, you don't take much time, and there's carpeting in the back of your van. And do you know what I did for you when I really started to like you? I made you a euphemism for every rent-boy's dream. I started it, and now all the boys say it, they say 'I'm off to wait for the fatman.' In ten years time, in twenty years, in a hundred years, when we're all dead, the rent-boys will still be telling each other they're off to wait for the fatman, with carpets in his van and pockets full of cash. I've made you legend." The boy now wore that expression that was more than laughter. He looked down at the fatman with adoration, half mock, half real, and placed his hands acquisitively around the fatman's head. "You're every rent-boy's dream, and I have you."

The dog yelped into the boy's long sigh. The boy looked toward the back door.

"No, you won't return him to Battersea. You'll finish him, and we'll bury him together."

"I can't," the fatman said, unable now to look into the boy's eyes. "I can't. I can't. 'E's all I 'ad. For so long 'e was all I 'ad."

The fatman felt the boy's hands leave his face, and then the rocking of the bed as the boy got off it. He watched the boy getting dressed, packing the few things he had into that long sailor's bag of his.

"I can't," he called out again as the boy left the bedsit.

17

SEAN DECIDED to do one more round of the station. By now all the boys knew him, and looked away from his car as he approached. He felt the complete emptiness of his search, like an insect that continues, by reflex, to perform some action long after it's dead. He was never going to find the boy. In some ways the boy had become now what he'd always been, a thing remembered, an ache in the past. The boy found his form in others, in their memories. And suddenly, through this fog of feeling, Sean thought of Caitlín, *her* form, that long hair like a kind of silt over her buried face, her body covert and sinuous, the coy way she ate, and it was really his wife he was thinking of, transposing tenderness — and more, much more, he realized, than tenderness; trying to find in Caitlín somewhere to place that burden of tenderness, to find in her form a way to feel more than impotence and anger, to find, perhaps, redemption. Sitting in her cabin that night, his mind had been fraught as always, setting up its spiteful dissonance. But he'd felt then what he felt now, his body wanting her, had let his body garner fragments for itself — the arch of her long foot, that slight flush of blood upon her chest, the well of her smooth, long neck. He'd allowed his body then, as he was allowing his body now, to remember that it could lose itself.

As he drove, he became lost in Caitlín-Rea's body, or rather, *found* his own body again in theirs. For the first time in years, he felt aroused, and it was while found in this arousal that his eyes caught the bare, lovely legs of a young woman, a girl really, standing on the street — a prostitute, her lips and eyes made up, but her bleached blonde hair almost crewcut. He looked up into her face and, meeting Sean's eyes, she gave that constrained smile that seemed to more than laugh, amazed but not surprised, because to someone in love, the object of that love is always expected.

It was a second before Sean could react. He was in the one-way system and there was nowhere to stop, taxis roaring past him. To a chorus of angry horns, he cut across three lanes, pulled his car up onto the pavement, and sprinted back along the street. There, in silhouette, the boy was still leaning against the lamppost. It was like those dreams of childhood, Sean's limbs suddenly leaden, but he was not trying to run away from, but toward his greatest fear. He'd found him. He *had* him. But when he was just yards from the boy, a gray van pulled up. The boy got in and the van drew away, driving right past Sean, close enough for Sean to slam his hand against the side of it.

Beside the boy, the fatman drove hunched over the wheel, tears streaming down his face, his whole body shaking. The boy lifted a hand to rub gently at the back of the fatman's neck, adjusted the wing mirror, and stared into it to look at Sean with a vague, pensive smile.

18

I WANT TO REMEMBER EVERYTHING. I'd been sad again, so sad Mum wanted me to try the medication the psychiatrist had given me. It was all secret because Dad wouldn't have me see a psychiatrist. He can't stand the failure. He still wants to fix me himself. He talks to me, he cries and wants to be responsible for my unhappiness. But I say to him, This is mine; this is the one thing I have. Durward came after Mum was gone, took the pills away, said that we must live in our own blood. Like ascetics in the desert, neither he nor I have eaten for days. We fool Mum and Dad, make sandwiches in front of them to take out with us, but feed them to the birds. It's to purify us. Durward lets me sleep only briefly, never a full night, wants to bring me into that place where the world of our dreams and of our consciousness fuse. It's as if he's cultivating my sadness into the most wonderful black flower.

I want to remember it. I was lying in bed, waiting for

him. So many times I've wanted to touch him. I've kept thinking of him emerging naked from the water; but I can never touch him, or even move my limbs toward him. I just can't.

So how do I remember it, this first time? How do I keep it, the dew left by his body? He got into bed beside me, as he's done many times before. He would sing gently that song of his, or talk, or read me parts of books and poems. We would lie close together, him behind me, but it always seemed as if there were a kind of electric field, a tender and unbearable static between us. And a few times I was brave enough to turn around, to face him in the dark, and though I longed to put my lips to his, to move my face that matter of an inch between us, he held that space, as if to feed my longing back into my sadness. So the strength of that longing became part of my sadness — enveined, ensinewed.

How do I remember it? There was something different. He lay on his back beside me and was breathing hard, smiling, beyond laughter, his eyes wild, unable to fix on anything. I know this. It's what happens sometimes before he goes into his sadness. It's as if he's been running, and there is still hope for escape, a euphoric hope, as if the running of a child in a game and the running of a child in a nightmare has been conflated, and he doesn't know whether to laugh or to scream. Breathing hard. The bed was knocking against the wall, making a sound like the ticking of a clock, and I realized that it was the beat of his heart, so powerful it thrust the whole bed against the wall. I wanted to touch him, but I couldn't. You can't. Not until he wants you to. He said he was afraid, because these were the happiest and most terrible moments of his life, that he could feel it coming on from within him, and was now more desperate and alive than he could ever be at any other time, aware of all his senses, his blood and breath, aware of everything he was to lose, as if a hand would come down and pluck out each nerve. Feel my heart, he said. I lifted my hand a little, but couldn't put it on him. So he took it and lay it on his heart. Can you feel it? Yes, I said. You can't feel it, he said, and pulled off his shirt. He told me to take off mine, and when I had, with his effortless strength he lifted me on top of him, held me into his body. The beat of his heart striking into my chest, he gently pulled back my hair.

How will I remember it, the moment he became lost in me?

19

IN ALEX'S ARMS, as they lay on the bed, the fatman cried abjectly for hours. The boy, with an oddly detached tenderness, held him until the fatman finally fell asleep. Then the boy slipped off the bed, opened the back door, and looked down at that pale smudge in the darkness, that fetal afterimage of light. On the floor in front of this lay the pickax handle the fatman had used.

The boy lifted the dog into his arms, that slack substance of life, its tongue lolling, and for a moment pressed his face into the dog's neck, inhaling its stale coat, getting its blood upon his cheek.

In the garden, as close to the oak tree as its roots would allow, he dug the grave, a hole like a well, narrow and deep. Sitting beneath the tree, he cradled the dog again, gently stroking its neck. Almost all night he sat in the cold, whispering to the dog. Finally, as dawn hazed the houses, he took the dog by its collar and lay himself across the soil so that he could lower it into the grave. He lay there a while longer, looking down at that pale conch.

Then he stood and took up a spadeful of soil. Holding it suspended, he looked down one last time.

"You and I, Feederboy," he said.

The boy showered in the house, then entered the sweltering room, which, over these past months, he'd filled with all manner of tropical plants. On the bed lay the fatman, naked but for the watches on his wrists, his face troubled even in sleep, and blossoming around him in the sheet, the stain of his sweat. In the room, there were now eight clocks. It was ten to seven. In ten minutes, they would all burst into sound. He went into the kitchen and whisked a dozen eggs with cream for the fatman's breakfast, and laid a dozen rashers and two slices of bread into the cold permanent lard of the saucepan on the stove.

He waited, looking from one to the other of the three clocks in the kitchen. Suddenly he seemed to remember something, the shock momentarily visible in his face. Quickly, he removed all trace of Feederboy: his bowls, all his food, his few rubber toys, the pictures of him, one hanging in the bathroom, another on the mantelpiece in the main room.

With just a few seconds to spare, the boy stood beside the bed and composed himself until the whole room was deluged with sound. The fatman jerked out of sleep, looking bewildered, pained, and the boy in a singsong voice said what he said to him every morning: "Up, up, up, darling. No rest for the wicked."

20

SEAN SAT IN HIS CABIN on the edge of his bunk, still afflicted by that glimpse he'd caught of the boy's face as he'd passed him in the street, that smile, that look of love. And that fatalism, as if the boy had been waiting there, unmoved, for all these years. "Finally you've come," his face had said. And still he had his beauty, beauty that worked its way inexorably into whatever wounds you carried. But what had shaken Sean most was that his glance at the boy had been a reflex of lust, which the boy must have seen in his face. Sean had been thinking of Caitlín and Rea, and with his body aroused for the first time in years, he'd caught those slender legs askance, had wanted to look into her eyes, had wanted that woman, that girl, to look into his. But it was the boy. Everything was the boy.

He heard Caitlín's old Volvo, with its broken muffler, pull up. His senses went to her, entered her, as she walked across the towpath, over the springy gangplank and onto the foredeck. As usual the university kids were up on the deck, and she must have stopped to talk to them, for he could hear their sudden laughter, two, three, four times, in unison, they

laughed uproariously. She was telling them a story, undoubtedly some ridiculous and mortifying predicament she'd
stumbled her way into. He could see her telling the story,
her slender body at once so expressive and constrained, her
large eyes narrowing cannily, widening with innocence.
And now, after tuning the slack time of those kids to a point
of clear resonance, she passed through them. From the
sound of her footsteps upon the floor of the main cabin
above him, Sean imagined her legs, conceived them, those
lovely, female legs, the boy's legs now Caitlín's legs. His
legs. Was she wearing those sheer white stockings? That
short black dress? He was inside her, saw what she saw, the
dark entrance to the short but precipitous stairway down to
the cabins. As she descended she noticed the light seeping
under his door. What did she feel? A frisson, a small and
unexpected subsidence beneath her heart? Walking to his
cabin, she smoothed down the sides of her dress, hefted
her heavy hair forward over her left shoulder, and finally
knocked. . . . Sean closed his eyes and felt a ghost of hope.

But the knock didn't come. He heard her open and shut
the door to her own cabin.

It surprised him, the profoundness of his disappoint-
ment, and how difficult it was to withdraw his senses from
her. For a moment he felt almost abject. But then he heard
her door open again, her rapid, resonant steps down the
hallway, and he called "Come in" perhaps even a fraction
of a second before her knock came.

She put her head around the door. There was no makeup
on her face, and her hair was tied back, which made her
look seventeen.

Narrowing her eyes at him in mock scrutiny, she said, "The air is thick with brooding."

"I'm wondering if I should go back home," he said.

Entering, she closed the door behind her and sat beside him on his bunk. She wore a baggy sweater and a pair of old jeans.

"God, you must be at least a foot too tall for this bed," she said.

"Too tall for this bed, too old for this boat, too tired to be chasing this boy."

"Chasing him?"

"Looking for him."

A frown flickered above her eyes. "I know there's something you're not telling me, but I'm not going to ask you."

"I need to find him. I need to find out something from him, and then I can go . . . go on." He looked at her as he amended his "go" to "go on," a look which told her that it did cost him to do this, that he was giving her something.

But the look she now returned frightened him, and in doing so quickened his feelings for her: it was a detached look, a look that comes not at the beginning of things, but at the end, when there's nothing left. It was a look barren, blind, insular, that he remembered from his wife in those fraught months after Megan's death, just before she left him.

"I'll take you to dinner," he said quickly.

Caitlín remained absorbed in this look for a moment, and then said in a tone that seemed to be giving him a chance, "All right."

21

THE INDIAN RESTAURANT was dark and completely empty, the waiter so softly spoken and respectful it was as if someone had died.

Caitlín had changed her clothes, put on makeup. She wore a pale, ribbed top and her long hair fell liquidly over the left side of her face.

She ran her finger down the condensation on her glass of white wine. "One time I was convinced my husband was having an affair. He told me he was doing a business course up at the South Bank University near his office after work every Thursday. And one Thursday evening I'd had dinner in town with a girlfriend of mine, and thought I'd try to catch him as he came out of class."

"But there was no class," Sean preempted.

"Oh no, my husband was far too meticulous for that. He'd even bought all the required books and would spend a few hours every weekend apparently studying. Anyway, I went to the class and glanced through the window — older people are so serious about learning, aren't they. It was like a whole room full of infants being rigorously toilet trained. But he wasn't there. So the next Thursday I borrowed my friend Jean's car and followed him after work. It was very exciting. I'd pulled my hair up into a huge woolen hat and wore a pair of outlandish glasses I'd found in Oxfam. I looked like a white Rastaferian librarian. So I followed him to the place of his tryst, which was this big council estate in Camden."

"The Windsor Estate?" Sean said.

"Yes, do you know it?"

"I did my final placement in Camden."

"So you'll know that it's the most dismal council estate in London. Isn't it funny how entrenched our class-consciousness is? I was so incensed that he was obviously having an affair with some East End peroxide slut, a woman who'd be your mistress for a bottle of stout and a box of Milk Tray once a week." (Sean was sure she could see in his face the quickened beat of his heart. He almost wanted to tell her to stop.) "I could even imagine their love-play, him vigorously aspirating every vowel like Edward Fox while she wantonly flung off every 'h'. I felt literally sick. From my car I watched him go up to the fourth floor. He knocked on a blue door right beside the stairwell. The door was opened, though I couldn't see by whom, and then he went in and remained there until the time his class would have ended. At home I'd left him a note to say that I'd gone out to comfort a heartbroken friend — which, I suppose, wasn't far from the truth — and when his car was gone I went right up to that door and hammered on it. Number 17, I remember, and that whole block stinking of lard and urine and cabbage. I didn't know what I was going to do when the woman opened the door. I probably would have just started crying. But, as you've guessed, it wasn't Barbara Windsor, it was an old man." (Relief. Sean's fear melted, dissolved.) "I told him I'd locked myself out of a friend's flat and wondered if I could use his telephone. He led me into the saddest, most dismal, most foul-smelling flat you could imagine. I once saw a bunch of dead, dried-out carnations on a grave, and that's what this place made me think of. He offered to make me a cup of tea, and I sat in the chair in which I knew my husband had also sat, a bare wooden chair. The sofa and the armchairs looked so filthy and beside the wooden chair there was a cup of tea that had gone cold. I made my fake telephone call and told the old man that I had to meet my friend downstairs in the parking lot in half an hour. I couldn't drink the tea he gave me either. It was so sweet and milky, and the cup smelled of grease. He had a pair of false teeth loose in his mouth and kept chewing on them. He smoked Woodbines, one after another. It was making me so nauseated. And he told me that it was a pity because I'd just missed his son, who would have driven me to my friend. And on the mantelpiece there were pictures of David — my husband — but only as a child and very young man. David had told me that his father had died. I asked the old man if his son was married, and he said no. I went to the bathroom just before I left, and that was the strangest thing. David's father had torn out the whole bath and sink — I assume he washed in the kitchen — and had put in an enormous chicken-wire cage filled with pigeons. The stench was unbearable, all those birds . . ."

"So what did you say to your husband?"

"I didn't say anything."

"Why?"

She pondered this for a moment. "I think because, in a way, it was too vast a lie to broach." She paused, still thinking. "And also . . . I think also that David, somehow, *was* that lie." She looked up at Sean with an intense and troubled appeal: "Does that make any sense?"

Sean nodded almost imperceptibly. He felt his face flush and wondered if she could see it in the dim restaurant light.

"Anyway," she concluded, "that lie became a part of the rot in our marriage. It ate away at every intimacy."

Both were silent for a while. Sean could hardly believe that he was here with this woman. The dim emptiness of the restaurant made him feel as if this were a rehearsal somehow in an empty theater. No, he'd not quite returned to life, but she was here, this woman, giving him a chance to rehearse that return. She'd made him feel, for the first time, something beyond his grief and fury, and the perfect thing, the most difficult thing, was that, like his wife, she too had been subject to the secret in the council estate, the lie in the marriage. And as they stared at each other, quite unabashedly, as if, for a moment, each had forgotten that he/she could be seen by the other, Sean realized that Caitlín was asking him to be honest.

"That's one reason I adored my wife so much," he began circuitously. "She had no capacity to lie. She never faked anything, not in our emotional life, not in our physical life, not in our spiritual life. She was a terrifying person really, an absolutist, an idealist. But it gave her such . . ." he spoke now with a hopeless intensity, pinching his fingers together, squinting his eyes, "a clarity. You could feel what she felt in every part of her. If you just touched her she rang . . . like a bulb of glass," he added more quietly, becoming self-conscious, "which was wonderful when things were good and awful when things were bad."

This wasn't enough, he knew; Caitlín was talking about the boy. He ordered two more drinks and waited until they arrived.

Then he said it. "The boy's my son. My real son, from an unfortunate relationship."

"While you were married?"

"No," he lied. "Before. I was very young." For a moment he felt terrified. It seemed to him that from just this, despite the lie, she would be able to unravel his whole life.

"So is this what you want to tell him?"

"In a way."

She seemed to realize that he'd given her a great deal and her look told him that she would, for now, demand no more. Progress had been made in the negotiation of their intimacy, a negotiation which, because they were past a certain age, a certain body of experience, could be done almost overtly.

Caitlín relaxed back in her seat with her glass of wine. "So why did you become a social worker?"

"God made me a social worker," Sean said, smiling, "because at one stage I wanted to rule the world. Now I'm ecstatic if there's enough milk in the office for my tea."

"You wanted to rule the world?" she said dubiously.

"Actually, I did. I was a very ambitious young man. I had a grand design for my life. I was trying to live the autobiography of a great man. I even had titles for it. "Reverence and Rage"; "The Boy from Bow." I invented countless personas. I was tough and I was sensitive and I was academic and I was bucolic. I was the perfect politician. It seemed to me that there was one glorious trajectory to one's life or there was nothing, a vast waste of nothing. And then, of course, when things don't quite work out, you find yourself living in the nothing."

"And you can bear that?" Caitlín asked, frowning a little, sad for him.

"It has its compensations," he said, looking up from his beer glass into her eyes. "A good Vindaloo not being the least of them."

She ignored his pathetic wit almost as a kindness to him, "So once you find the boy — if you find him — are you going to make him part of your life?"

"No. He will be a kind of closure." Then with a vehemence that verged on anger, he said, "Caitlín, I've made so many mistakes."

He'd been leaning in toward her, but now sat back, as she had. He'd said enough, and she conceded this with a contrite glance.

The waiter came to take their plates and to bring them some steaming flannels. Sean ordered another drink for them both.

"So, he's your son," Caitlín said, musing for a moment, but then adding quickly, as if to assure him that she was not meaning him to say any more, "Funny because do you remember when you first came into the home, when I first met you and you told me I reminded you of someone?"

Sean nodded.

"And I said, 'Don't tell me your ex-wife.' And you said, 'Yes, but she was lovely . . .'"

Sean waited.

"Well, on the day before Devon ran away from the home, I was brushing my hair in the hallway mirror. I'd been there for perhaps ten minutes. And when I finally turned to leave, there was a click and a flash. Devon was standing in the hall about a yard from me. He'd taken a photograph. I don't know how long he'd been there. I hadn't heard him approach. It gave me such a shock, and I would have been angry except that he looked really troubled. I'd never seen him like that. I could actually take hold of his face. It was the first time I was able to really look into his eyes. And just a moment after I'd seen him, he told me that he was sorry he hadn't had a chance to get to know me. I said that there was still time. Stupid. I should have realized he was going to run away. And then he said exactly what you said, that I reminded him of someone. And being my tactful self, I said, 'Don't say your mother.' He said, 'Foster mother, but she was wonderful.' Exactly what you said, *exactly*. Now, of course, I realize that you were both talking about the same woman. But then he said that he was sorry, and he seemed *really* sorry; and I said, 'What for?' and he said, 'I'm sorry that you remind me of someone.' Said it as if this were so terrible, tragic even. And then something in his look really frightened me. I mean, talking of honest people, he's terrifyingly honest. He has a naked face. And I think that when we look at anything that's really naked we just can't believe it — which is what can be so compelling and so repulsive about any kind of nakedness. I remember Ronan once said that though Devon was obviously incredibly talented and wonderful in so many ways, that he sometimes got the most overwhelming sense of evil from him. He described him as a changeling. Ronan has that Catholic sense of evil as something protean and formless, a lie. But evil is also the knowledge of more than we've been designed to know. And I think if Ronan got a sense of evil, it was because Devon's face was that. It was more than we should ever know. But I never got a sense of evil from him — a portentousness, yes — but not evil. I think perhaps because I could never see him older than his beauty would last. And the night of that same day, the night he ran away, I dreamed about him — which is strange because people never go directly into my dreams. It can sometimes take years for them to bubble up to the surface, and even then they're often inside another face. But he looked exactly as he'd looked in the hallway. I was in some forest somewhere, walking toward him. He was sitting in a sort of clearing on the other side of a dense tunnel of foliage; and as I entered it, I realized that he was much farther away than it had seemed at first. And suddenly it was completely dark, and Devon was no longer at the end of the tunnel, and I wanted, desperately, *desperately,* to go back, but I'd already gone too far. . . . That was a terrible dream."

She put her empty glass down as she finished speaking, and Sean paid the bill.

They walked in silence along the bank of the Thames, stopping once to look at a couple of ghostly cranes. As the boat came into sight, Sean felt a tremor of panic.

He slowed their already ambling pace even further. "Have I got into your dreams yet?" he asked.

"All I can say is that the audition went well," she said. "It's very likely that you're in, but I can't promise you a major part."

He smiled. His tongue felt leaden.

Caitlín went quickly on, "But the director is corruptible — she's notorious in fact." She gave him a canny look, and their eyes stayed together for a while.

"And there's a really good part coming up in the next show."

"Would I suit it?"

She sighed meditatively. "You're not perfect. The director has tended to go for rather skinny men — the sort of heroin addict physique."

"What about age?"

"Well, she's no spring chicken herself and you're well preserved, good foundation. Doesn't look as if you'll sag too soon. And I'll let you in on a little secret," she said, taking hold of his sleeve to bring him to a stop. He took her hand. She whispered, "She does find you very attractive, but that's just between you and me." She laughed, with an odd shyness, and pulled her hand gently out of his. It was as if she were suddenly frightened, and walked quickly on ahead.

For once no one was out on deck. She was waiting for him in the musty main cabin. He brought himself to a stop in front of her, close, but she looked troubled, stared up into his eyes almost angrily as he put his hands on her arms. He kissed her gently, but she was only half responsive.

"What's wrong?" he said.

"I'm not your wife," she said.

22

"I CAN'T TASTE ANYTHING. That damn stuff stops me from tasting anything," Ronan's mother complained as he nosed the needle into the sore, thin skin of her arm.

"You don't understand," Ronan persisted, his placating tone riding precariously upon the back of his desperation. "I have so much — *so much* to do today. Red tape all morning at social services, and then I have meetings with sponsors all afternoon. I can't get out of it. So is it too much — just today — for me to ask you to take your own medication? Everything's ready. All you have to do is take it, and take it *on time*." He tried to force these words into her fisted face as he drew out the needle.

"One needle exactly at one," he continued, "one at three, and one at six. I'll be back before nine. The clock is all set. It will sound each time you need to do it. You have done this before. You *have* done it before. There won't be anyone here at all. Theresa's gone on a retreat for the whole weekend and Caitlín has taken the boys to Brighton. She won't be back until at least eight." Ronan could feel his mouth going dry as her face clenched more tightly into its recalcitrance.

"I'd call you, but I know you won't pick it up. I'd get the home help to come in, but I know you won't answer the bloody door." He began to lose his temper. "They said if they have to call the police to break in again, they'd insist you go into a home. Did you hear that? You'd have to go into a home."

"Don't you shout at me," she suddenly yelled. "Don't you dare shout at me. Do you know what you did to me?"

He sat heavily down on her bed, covering his face with his hands. "Oh, for the love of God."

"The love of God?" she took up with vicious fury. "The love of God? Well, it wasn't the love of *God* that made you a priest, was it?"

He felt numb.

"Do you know what you did to me? My father owned —"

"Pubs, potatoes, and peat bogs!" he shouted her down. "Your father was the king of Ireland — him and every other drunken navvy in Kilburn."

"It was your father in you," she said. "*His* blood." Without even the usual preliminaries, she'd gone straight to the most vicious thing she could say.

They were like two prizefighters, and these were the last rounds. Battered, they drew each telegraphed blow from their depleted wells.

After a moment, Ronan said coldly, mechanically, knowing that it was useless anyway, knowing that he had no choice but to return before one: "Now you remember what the doctor said. If you inject them before time, it could bring on a stroke. You could get brain damage. Then you'll just be in a home, and you won't be able to speak or watch television or anything. And if you don't take it you know what'll happen."

Yes, he would have to be back before one; and now it was almost ten-fifteen. He got up to go and stood for a moment at the door. Her life for this one day was laid out before her: the small microwave and refrigerator for her food, the three syringes, the telephone with all the emergency numbers, the emergency beeper. There she sat like something blocking the throat of her own life, choking herself. All her suffering had turned to bile. Despite himself, his guilt rankled. She was his guilt, which he kept in this room, constantly alive, as if he were nurturing a vengeful ghost. If he'd deserved it, that would be one thing, but to those women who'd come to him in his capacity as a priest, his intentions had always been good, replete with sympathy and love. What had he done that he should be so punished? Just one of them he'd kissed, and so innocently, a matter of one moment in his life. Just one kiss. He'd loved her in all her grief, had loved her sad and sordid life, had kissed that, had kissed through her into the dingy rooms and the sodden, heavy men, closing over her like the loam of years, and the musk and the soiled walls, and the moaning and the mindless. If it was lust, it was lust for the brevity of her sensual life, for her short flowering before she became bruised, bloated, and child-ridden, a lust for drunkenness and a heavy somnambulistic conception, men flinging their dice beneath her, into her. He'd kissed her badly dyed hair, the bleach she used to hide a downy mustache, kissed the heavy makeup, the cheap perfume, and the clothes that held her sex in shape, kissed the coy flick of her hair and her mindless devotion to God. This he'd kissed, kissed it as tenderly, reverently, as he might have kissed God.

But that woman had seen his intentions quite differently, and she'd told people that he'd taken advantage of her. His rough congregation had always disliked him for his teetotaling fastidiousness, for the plum his mother had put into his mouth, for the Eton English with which he delivered sermons he considered theological tours-de-force, himself a budding Aquinas. In Acton, of all places! How young he'd been. So all those lies had sprung up about the women he'd seduced, the children he'd molested — all of it from that one kiss. And his mother who, at his ordination, had managed to recoup something of her pride, the mother now of a priest, her son proof positive of her superiority to the rabble with whom she'd been forced to live, had then had that pride stripped away, like a new wound at the very place of a barely healed old wound, the pain multiplied because her son had been so faultless she'd never had to trouble to love him. Just for that kiss, the impulse of a young man to touch the body of God, everything had been lost.

For these past weeks, he hadn't been able to stop thinking about Hilary — that hot dismal basement, her brutish husband, her desire to educate herself, her need for him, all that he could give her. He now remembered all those others the boy had been so perfectly: Bethany, who lived with her invalid father; Andrea, that hard woman who'd dispatched her lunch in front of him in Hyde Park, her unhappiness mute, absolutely unavailable, expressed only in her sensuality, in which she was released, and after which she closed again; and the angry, insomniac eyes of Fiona, whose hands were shaking as she'd asked him for a light on the steps of the British Museum. What would his life be without the boy? He'd have nothing. Theresa, his mother, and a handful of remembered assignations to suckle from until they were dry. Then he too would be dry, blowing around the city in his coat, looking for the sad women.

He'd really thought he'd lost the boy forever this time. Two months had gone by, but this morning he'd found that sweet note on his doormat, telling him to meet her in the library of City University, where she, on his advice (spelled "advise"), and keeping it secret from her husband, was auditing a course on Rilke. She wanted to talk to him a little about Rilke and about the book he'd suggested to her, *Justine*, which she'd found so lovely, but so difficult.

Ronan was at the university library by eleven. He knew that he should get back to his mother by one, but that he had some leeway, that even three wouldn't be too late. Hilary had given him the number of a carrell, but had forgotten to tell him which floor she'd be on, and the carrel numbers were the same on each floor except prefixed with the floor number. Almost running, he went through the carrels of each floor in turn, his longing for her, just to see her, parching his throat. It was the half-term break and the library was almost completely empty. Finally, he arrived at the fifth floor, which was closed for actual lending, a warehouse for damaged books and periodicals to be bound. All around the walls ran exposed pipes. The ceiling was damaged in a number of places and the air was filled with the smell of rotting paper. At the end of a long corridor of carrels, he could see one with a light on. Rather than walking directly to it, Ronan walked the length of one set of bookshelves and then down the next aisle, so that he could see the lit carrel directly on, from a distance. Thus he quietly approached down a corridor of books, she in her cage at the end, in her cell of light, bent over her work, utterly absorbed, as if she'd forgotten he was even coming. He managed to reach almost to the point where he could touch her before, with a start, throwing her hand against her chest, she glanced up.

"Oh, how lovely to see you," she said, her tone oddly formal as she kissed him lightly on the cheek and self-consciously smoothed down her clothes.

"I was just reading the . . . these elegies," she said, obviously fearing to mispronounce them.

"Ah, the Duino Elegies," he said, quoting — "'For beauty is nothing but the beginning of terror which we still are just able to endure, and we are so awed because it serenely disdains to annihilate us.'"

"He's wonderful," she said.

"Yes. There's one poem you must read, called 'The Headless Torso of Apollo,' with a last line that I think only Rilke could have conceived and got away with: 'For here there is no place that cannot see you. You must change your life.'"

She'd shuffled that initial coldness off a little, and looked lost in Ronan for a moment, lost with a longing for all he knew, raw in her young breast the sense of infinity in these words. But the only thing quick in Ronan himself was his longing for her, the intimation of infinity in her guileless eyes, in her need and desire for him, in the way her cheap perfume mingled with the smell of moldering books, this rot of words.

"So how is your class going?" he said.

"Oh, I feel like such a fool. I don't know anything. There are a couple of women who laugh at me when I ask questions. I know they're stupid questions."

"I'm sure they're not. That's horrible," he said, resting his hand paternally on her arm. Though she didn't exactly shrink from his touch, he sensed that she wasn't yet ready for it and quickly removed his hand.

After a slightly awkward moment, she said, "There's this lovely guy there — Peter. He works for the gas board, but he's really read a lot. Not as much as you, of course," she added hastily. "You probably know more than the teacher. But he's sort of taught himself. We have a real laugh at the breaks. We're going to study together. He's going to help me out with writing the essays."

Ronan tried to stop his smile from congealing upon his lips. She seemed to become aware of his discomfort and, glancing away, toyed nervously with her earring.

"I want to talk to you about *Justine*," she said, taking a breath. "There's a sort of reading room just down at the end of the stacks. We could go in there."

"Of course," he replied, feeling suddenly hollow, the sight, as she removed a copy of *Justine* from her bag, of her slender neck, her lips, the fringe of her blonde hair, sapping him of his will. He followed her down the corridor. She was wearing a jean skirt, white pumps, and a baggy pink sweater.

As they entered the small room, which contained a large desk, half a dozen chairs, and stacks of magazines bundled and ready to be bound, he brought himself to say, "I have to be back at the home by three — at the latest."

She frowned — a hard, stubborn frown. "Why?"

"It's my mother, I . . . I need to give her her medicine."

"That's why you left me the last time."

"She's very ill."

"But I so wanted to thank you," she said, "for helping me. I'm marinating some chicken. I thought I'd make you dinner. My husband, he's on a long haul to Cologne."

"Well, I could go back, check on her, and then come straight to your flat," he said.

"For how long?" she protested, her frustration turning to anger. "A few hours? Until you have to go back to your mother?"

"She's a difficult woman. She's had a very hard life."

Worse than anger or accusation, she now looked disappointed, her eyes working over his face as if she were beginning to reassess his infallibility.

"It's all right," she said with a cold determination. "I'll

call Peter. I promised I'd have him round for dinner some-
time anyway."

"No," he said. "No, I'd really like to come. . . . I . . . it's
just . . ."

"It's all right," she repeated, absently toying with the
book in her hands. He saw now that its pages were riddled
with bookmarks. These were places at which she had questions for him, and the sight of this need for him in her small
hands made him feel the loss of her as the loss of any hope
in his life. And he knew that if he lost this one, he would
lose them all.

"Look, I really want to come," he pleaded.

"I've bought you something." She was almost inaudible.
"It's at home. I wanted to give it to you after dinner." She
glanced at her watch. "Look," she said with a surge of
hopeful energy. "It's only twelve. Come back with me. I'll
make you a quick lunch. I'll give it to you, and then you
can go."

"You don't understand," he said, putting his hand paternally on her arm.

But she shrugged him off and began to move toward the
door. He quickly snatched up her wrist, causing her to drop
the book.

Prone and open, *Justine* lay like a small violence between
them.

"*Please,*" he said. "Understand."

Pulling her wrist free, she squatted to pick up the book.

"All right," he said, taking her arms in his hands as she
stood. "I'll come."

He thought she'd still be angry, but she was actually

crying. He embraced her more fully, and in this motion quickly checked his watch. It was closer to twelve-thirty than twelve, and under his breath, as he held Hilary into him, he cursed his mother.

By the time they'd got to that strange, hermetic room, hot and humid, full of plants, it was almost one-thirty. On the journey, she'd become lighthearted again, girlish, excited, and on entering the bedsit she kicked off her shoes so they flew across the room. At the foot of the bed she'd set a small card table for dinner with flowers, candles, and a bottle of red wine. Beside one of the plates sat a small wrapped package. She lit the candles and switched off all the other lights.

"It'll take me just a minute to cook this food," she said.

He glanced at her bare feet, her lovely young legs.

"I really — " he started meekly to protest, but she ran up to him and pulled his coat down off his shoulders.

"Come on," she said, tugging at his sweater, "take this off."

He tried to kiss her, but she turned away, laughing playfully.

"No, no, no," she said. "Not yet." And now she looked up at him steadily, beautifully, putting her hand on his brow and saying, "You're like so many men. You want to finish before you've begun. You know so much, but you know nothing about pleasure." Touching the edge of her lip to his, she pulled off his sweater and, ignoring his protests, removed his heavy watch, placing it beside one of the three clocks on the mantelpiece.

"Open that wine," she said, and ran into the kitchen.

A few moments later she came in with the starter — prawn cocktail. It was perfect, Ronan thought, just what she *would* choose, the ingénue's sense of sophistication.

They sat, a strange numbness overcoming his limbs as he poured the wine.

"Cheers," she said, lifting her glass to him.

In a silence tremulous with her nervousness, they ate the starter.

After they'd finished, she said, "I know you have to go now."

"I — "

"It's all right," she quickly reassured him, "but please just open your present before you go."

It was a signed first edition of *Justine*.

"This must have cost you a fortune."

"Do you like it?"

"Of course."

She took his hand, her face becoming serious. "You can't stay just a little longer?" she asked.

It was as if a part of his mind had been anesthetized. He leant over the table and now she let him kiss her, let him come round to her, almost knocking the little table over, let him pull her sweater up over her head, let him fall roughly into her.

23

IT HAD BEEN DARK for a long time before Ronan returned to the home. After he'd left Hilary's flat at five, he'd sat for a couple of hours down by the river, and had then caught the bus back. Caitlín and the boys had not returned yet, and the place was completely quiet. In the hallway he stood for a moment, taking the institution into his lungs. There was nothing of him in it. It did not know him. His home was gone.

He took off his hat and coat, but didn't know why. Where was there to hang them in the hallway? So he put them back on again, then listened; no sound. Some minutes later, slowly, he made his way upstairs. The blue light of the mute television flickered beneath her door. He lifted his hand to check the time, but his watch was gone. He opened the door. She sat listing to one side in her chair, illuminated by the silent television, a great bloom of saliva on her blouse. He let out a moan of which he was hardly aware. Nothing had been touched, the syringes full, everything as he'd left it. Without entering, he closed the door, leaning his head against it and moaning again, his body dawning with relief.

24

May 20th

I CAN HEAR MUM CRYING, crying and shouting, and Dad, his voice, his body subduing her. What use is there to feel now, he's saying in his thunderous rumble from the mountain, what use is there in feeling for the broken boy? It's as if by the slow action of a screw his voice is tightening a steel band around my head. I saw him die. We took him out, Durward and I. We didn't force him. Durward gave him the choice. Of course he came. The three of us, we went through the woods, down to our secret hut in the quarry, and then up a steep bank of scree to get to the forest. I could see that Liam was having trouble. His face flushed, he gulped the air like a fish in dirty water. The avalanched scree made the air thick with lime. Even I could hardly breathe. And after the scree a precipitous climb up a bank of clay. I tried to help my brother, but Durward stopped me, and he and I used exposed roots to pull ourselves to the top. Finally safe, we looked down at Liam, who'd scaled the scree to the bottom of the clay cliff, but now just stared up at us, stared up as if he were the one we would have to leave behind, as if he were still in the river to the bank of which we'd made it, the water rising to his gasping mouth. And approaching him through the water, I could see the wakes of those nightmares that rise from the depths with their teeth. Durward called down, "Whatever does not kill us. If it is the end, move into it. Love it."

I saw some understanding pass between them, a moment of extreme love that excluded me so completely I felt it almost as a blow. My brother, his face horribly distorted with the effort, began to climb toward us, his frail body, clambering, like a wet spider. Almost unconsciously I was calling softly, crying, Liam, Liam, words unattached to will, they neither told him to stay nor to climb, but were the purest grief, so much lighter than the air they might have lifted me into the sky and made of me a constellation. And when he was just a few feet away from us both, clutching to a root, his face crimsoned as if the blood were broken, his teeth ground, his body shuddered. I moved nearer to him, reaching down my hand. But Durward, with his effortless strength, took hold of me, embraced me, and both of us stared at our brother, as he slid down the rock face as if he'd liquefied, as if those nightmares had taken hold of him, had drawn him back, his mouth open, but the air like a rock he was trying to force into his throat. His face the color of blood. I saw him seize, a stream of saliva run from his lips, darken the ground.

We carried his body back, cleaned it in the bath as tenderly as if he were our baby. Then we dressed him and lay him in his bed, as quietly as the dead.

Durward told me that he would call the ambulance and then my father, that I should go upstairs and lie down. I was so tired, so tired from all these days of sleeplessness, that my brother's death became a kind of membrane around my sleep, unreal, half remembered, like something from another life, or the fear of something yet to come. And the ambulance, and the heavy feet running about the house, and the first scream of my mother, all of it weaving, becoming the cocoon that replaced my sleep, for I was too tired to sleep. My brother was dead.

25

THE FATMAN SAT ON THE BED, his back to the footboard, sweat peeling from his red, ingenuous face. He was holding the photograph the boy had taken of Caitlín standing in the hallway of the boy's home, her face empty, her eyes reddened by the camera's flash. The boy sat exactly opposite him, his back to the headboard. The soles of their feet were pressed together. Both were naked, but the fatman now wore three watches, the boy having added Ronan's to the other two.

"I've never told anyone but you what they did to me," the boy said. "And you would hardly believe it when you see her. Butter wouldn't melt in her mouth. She smells of baking and starched sheets. But he, my foster father, was never even half as vicious — as viciously inventive — as she was. It would have shocked Myra Hindly what she came up with."

"Why didn't you go to the social services?" the fatman asked meekly, looking down with a grimace into the photograph.

"For God's sake, I was eleven," the boy said, exasperated. "And my foster father *was* the social services. He'd
prepared for everything, had written up all these reports
that claimed I had profound emotional misunderstandings
of intimacy and the intentions of any physical contact what-
soever, that I'd been in the system so long I knew exactly
how to manipulate it for my own ends, that I had socio-
pathic tendencies which he believed he might be able to
reverse, that I had no real understanding of the distinction
between lie and truth, and that I'd been so rejected and
marginalized that I used lies to place myself at the focus of
attention." The boy pressed his fingers to his eyes as if he were
about to cry, but contained himself, and continued more
calmly. "On top of this, of course, which is maybe the most
difficult thing for you to understand, I really loved him. I
really loved him," he emphasized, as if still amazed himself.
"And her too. I *had* nothing else; I'd *known* nothing else."

"I can't believe they did those things to you," the fatman
suddenly shouted, his jaw trembling, a tear leaking from his
right eye. Then, more quietly, "I can't believe they did that
to you."

"You say that the thing that makes you most miserable is
that it doesn't seem as if I can ever really love you, that I
seem so often so far away. Well this is why. Because I don't
live in my senses. When it was happening, when my foster
father and mother were doing those things to me, to survive I would imagine myself — my body — as immortal.
But all my feelings of love, my emotions, all those things
that might weaken me, I consigned to this other person.

This other person embodied my capacity for love — do you understand? I never saw this person. This person was like someone in a dream, when you're in a house alone at night and it's raining and you know someone is in the house with you. And as you move through the house you find places where they've just been, the impression they've made in a seat, a half-drunk glass of wine. Then you hear the closing of a door somewhere." The boy paused. "Since then I've been searching for this person. I imagine sometimes that I'll search until the world ends. Then I'll float in space, waiting for that same confluence of conditions that will remake the world — impossible, but I can wait forever, until it all happens again. Then I'll fall to Earth. Just volcanoes and black oceans, but I'll know that somewhere that person who will contain every real feeling I could ever have for another is beginning to be woven from rings of amino acids. And I'll wait, watch it all, the first creatures in the oceans, the dinosaurs, the first humans, each civilization as it flourishes and falls . . ."

The boy took a heavy breath, closed his eyes. The fatman crawled over to him, tried to embrace him, but the boy pushed him away as if his skin were too sensitive to touch.

"I can't be anything that is whole until they're gone," the boy said, more coldly now. "I can't love you. I can't love until they're gone, until I've taken it in my hands to finish them. And do you know what's worse — what's worse is that I found out a few days ago that they're going to foster more children."

The boy stared at the fatman for a moment. "If it's not

just for me, if you can't just help me, then think of them. Will you help me?" the boy asked.

The fatman's eyes flinched. He looked pained, almost fevered, licking his dry lips and swallowing.

The boy reached over and picked up Caitlín's photograph, looking into it, but holding it so the fatman could see it also.

"Don't even think of her as something human," the boy continued gently. "She's not. People do sell their souls. They live like vampires, the two of them. They're irredeemable. Do you remember that novel I read you, where he loved that girl, but she became a vampire, and he had to kill her — *he had to* because of what she was doing to those children. And I promise you, when she sees you, she'll seem so sweet. Don't look into her eyes. She'll beg you. She'll seem so human. Just remember this face, and the face in that *Tales from the Crypt,* just remember how it suddenly transforms. Only the soulless can seem that genuine; only the soulless can transform so quickly." The boy put the photograph down on the bed, then reached over and gently touched the fatman's cheek. "Look at me," he said. The fatman, who was staring at the photograph, his face wrought with anxiety, now looked up at the boy.

"I've told you this so many times," the boy continued, "and it's true. All these things in our dreams, they're real — real people: vampires, werewolves, demons, changelings, and either they act in the night or they wait for a change in the world that will turn a cab driver into a colonel, a painter into a dictator, a butcher of meat into a butcher of men." The boy leaned forward as if reaching, but at once pushed his delicate white hands against the fatman's chest. "Do you understand me? I can never give myself until this is done. I can never be happy until this is done. This woman has no soul."

The fatman stared feverishly into the boy's face, which remained adamant with the truth of what he'd said.

"But do I just 'it 'er? What if she's not there? What if she don't die? 'Ow can I tell if she's dead? 'Ow can I tell?"

"You'll know if she's dead, and you must make sure she is. She's not going to wait for very long so you must be there exactly at eight and it's not easy to get there. It's in a quarry and the nearest the road puts you is a few miles away. And if you fail, then I'm gone forever. Do you understand? Because I'm going to kill the man at the same time, at exactly eight o'clock in that brewery in London and if I kill him and you don't kill her, she'll tell the police that it was me, and she'll have the evidence on me. . . . Bury her deep and you'll bury all the badness in my life, in our life, and you'll bury too all the bad things you've done, you'll bury what happened with that boy — "

"You said you'd never bring it up again," the fatman shouted. "It was the only time. I've never done anything like that again. I've — "

"It's all right," the boy cut in. "Now you have a chance to bury it, with her, with all the badness of our lives because you're not bad. Your heart is clean but for that one thing. With her death you can bury it. And then you and I can live free. We'll move. I want to move from here. We'll move to

Cornwall, away from this stinking city. I've seen the place where we can live." The boy's face was now so close to the fatman's. "This coming week, on Thursday night we'll do it both at the same time, at eight o'clock exactly, and it'll be a consummation. Do you know what that means?"

The fatman shook his head.

"It means that when we do it, I will become part of you and you will become part of me. You will become that person I've been looking for, and you'll never have to worry about being alone. Look at your watches. What time is it?"

The fatman lifted up both his wrists. All three watches showed that it was now eight o'clock.

"Eight," he said, amazed.

"Eight exactly," the boy said, and kissed him.

26

THE CAR DROPPED Ricky off under the train arches. He spat a few times onto the pavement and put an Opal Fruit into his mouth. He had enough money now for a saveloy and chips, a pack of fags, and he needed to get some foundation in the morning from Boots because he could feel more cold sores coming up just beneath his nose. But that would leave him with nothing again. He shivered and pulled his sagging cardigan tighter around him. It smelled of old people. He thought of his grandfather making chip butties for them both every evening. As they ate them, his grandfather would continue reading the racing pages while Ricky watched *Are You Being Served?* looking closely at their faces because his mother was the one who did them — even Mrs. Slocum's fluorescent hair. But he hadn't been able to stand it there anymore, his grandfather's snoring, the grease all over the kitchen, making it sticky when you walked, and that school where they called him dingle, and his teacher, Bellamy, that bitch, with her little face frowning, keeping him after class and talking to him about how to brush his teeth and keep himself clean. He would fantasize all the time — still did — of renting a little room in the middle of nowhere, leaving everything. He imagined himself as a grotesque and crippled man, a hunchback in a wheelchair. And in this room he would create a beautiful human machine, flesh and nerves on the outside, so he could still feel, but the skeleton an indestructible metal. The machine would look like that man in the Boss advert in that magazine he'd found, who had eyes like Priestly's. He'd then invent a device that could transfer him into this body, his soul, his memories, leaving his own weak diseased body behind, as a snake leaves its skin.

A terrible pain shot through Ricky's teeth, and spitting out the Opal Fruit he scrunched up his face for a moment before delving gingerly with his finger into his mouth. Closing his eyes, he pressed hard onto one of his molars and let out a feeble moan, a stream of saliva coursing down his chin. He dug into his mouth a little more, and when he finally pulled his finger out, it was covered with blood. He had to remember that he mustn't eat anything on the right side of his mouth now.

The gauzy rain was only apparent in the halos of the streetlamps, but he was almost soaked through and nuzzled himself into the shallow hollow of the bricked-in arch.

He needed to save some money. He needed to get out of the country, to get to somewhere where there was sun. Priestly had often talked to them about California, about all of them, the boys, driving the whole length of this road called Route 1: the ocean, wildflowers, cliffs, San Francisco, L.A., mountains full of redwoods and eucalyptus, their bark peeling them naked, and fog rolling in from the ocean. We'd all have a house, Priestly had said, in the mountains, and one by the ocean. Yes, Ricky thought, somewhere where there was sun and he could finally get away from his grandfather, the smell of his old flesh, the smell of grease, the stinking toilet that they had to flush with a bucket, those thick, undercooked chips on wet white bread covered in the black imprints of his grandfather's fingers from the ink on his newspaper.

"Shit, fuck," Ricky shouted, foul saliva welling in his mouth again. "Christ," he called out as he spat a bloody, phlegmy gob and the rain began to come down even harder. He would get on a plane. He would go to California, would find some real work and get this stench out of his nostrils, this taste out of his mouth. But even as he thought this, he pulled the cardigan tighter and drank it in, distilled it, the quickened smell of old men, of the gray streets of London.

"Fuck," he shouted, just for the bitter pleasure of it, the transgressive strangeness because one thing he dimly remembered was that his mother's one rule — perhaps it's what made her feel like a mother — was that he must never swear, as if that were the root of all evil.

"Shit, fuck, Christ!"

Then, with a shock, he saw it, the aura of bleached hair, now long, the dark figure beneath the lamplight.

"Priestly!" Ricky got up and scrambled over to him. For how long had he been there watching him with that smile of his? He'd come out of nowhere. Hope returning, life returning, he stared up with canine anticipation into Priestly's lovely face.

"Saint," Priestly said, resting his hand tenderly on the side of Ricky's neck, "why are you cursing the rain?"

It was pouring now, both of them soaked, water streaming from their faces, the light from the streetlamp above them illuminating the great dark arches of the railway bridge. Ricky no longer shivered with the cold, but with anticipation, remembering the last time he'd seen Priestly, who'd turned up on the day before Christmas in that alley where the boys would sit sometimes. He'd brought with him a whole supermarket trolley of the most fantastic food, which he'd somehow "borrowed" from Marks and Spencers: cooked chickens and cheesecakes and champagne and strawberries. And Ricky was included in the feast. None of the boys were ever cruel to him when Priestly was around, or even called him bad names, because Priestly, for some reason, had dubbed him "Saint," a name some of the boys still used for him. His feeling on seeing Priestly then was like the feeling he had now, electric, the sense that something incredible was going to happen. When Priestly wore that smile of his, you realized that anything was possible. It was a little like the feeling Ricky got sometimes when he lost himself in his human-machine fantasy, when he was looking down from within beauty, power, immortality at that grotesque body he'd left behind. In that smile was California too, the wildflowers and the cliffs and the mountains, the ocean, as if Priestly were impermeable to ugliness, had never been touched by it, and could conceive only of beauty, could bring a feast to an alleyway of lost boys, could give them dream names, could gather them, as one gathers coins from the gutter, running them beneath the spatter of a broken drainpipe until they gleamed. Standing here in the rain, the jealous rain running the streetlight down his exquisite face, as if the rain were nothing. He'd come from nowhere. Only Priestly could do that.

"I wasn't cursin' it," Ricky said, smiling. "You back then?"

"For a while maybe?"

Suddenly Priestly glanced off into the darkness, as if he'd seen something, his face anxious.

"Where you stayin' then?" Ricky said.

Warily, Priestly turned back to him. "There's a derelict brewery by the river. You know it: I took you and some of the boys to stay there one night after we'd seen the Smiths at Hammersmith Odeon."

"Down Mortlake way?"

"Yes."

"Opp'sit the boat 'ouse?"

"That's it."

"Why you stayin' all the way down there then?"

"It's got old memories. And I'm only staying there tonight and tomorrow night. I think I might have another place on Friday."

"With the fatman?"

"No. Another man. Been after me for a long time . . ." Priestly's voice trailed off. Again, he looked out anxiously into the darkness, in a way that made Ricky think of a beautiful dog, not seeing, but hearing, smelling, sensing something that no one else could.

Ricky, starving to speak, took his opportunity. "My

mum's now working on Eastenders right. She does all of
'em; she even does the men too, like, like I told you she
did Russ Abbot, right, for *Oliver* and now she does Susan
Tulley and Anita Dobson. She goes out for drinks with 'em
and stuff and one time she told me Anita Dobson said — "

"I thought you were getting out of here?" Priestly said, as
if Ricky wasn't even speaking.

"I 'ad some dosh but it got nicked."

"What about all that money I gave you?"

"Just went," the boy said.

Priestly looked sadly down at him. "What about California?" he said. "I don't want to go on my own, but I can't
pay for everyone."

"I'm definit'ly goin'. My mum'll give me some money for
my birthday."

"Stop it," Priestly said softly. "Stop lying."

He took hold of Ricky's cardigan by the collar, pulled
him closer, and firmly, coldly, he said, "You're going to die
in this stinking cardigan in some pissy stairwell."

"I ain't got no fuckin' money," Ricky screamed, tearing
himself away.

Ricky stared down at the pavement, furious, trembling,
at the verge of tears. His eyes wide, he looked like the
child he was. After a moment, he couldn't bear it any longer
and glanced up. But that was even more unbearable, for it
struck him now, for the first time, that Priestly was almost a
man. He looked back down into the pavement.

After a moment, Priestly pulled from his trouser pocket a
crumpled twenty-pound note and handed it to Ricky.

"Take it," he said.

"I'm not fucking lying," Ricky shouted, spittle sparking from his mouth, his face crimsoning, his little fists bunched and white.

"Get something to eat."

"I'm not fucking lying," Ricky screamed now, his face a crying face but without the tears, only fury, fury seizing his simple mechanism.

Unseen to Ricky, for Ricky kept staring rigidly down into the ground, Priestly's face flickered, almost flinched, as if something sharp and solid, some scruple, were passing down his throat.

His face hardened. Coldly he said, "You're a liar. I know your mother. Your mother's that slag who cleans the toilets in the Queen's Arms. I've seen her in there drinking snakebites. Paralytic. And she's been fucked by every navvy drunk enough to do it."

Stunned nearly out of his fury, Ricky looked up into Priestly's face, expecting cruelty but seeing none; and seeing no beauty. Priestly looked old, as old as his grandfather. In his face was a despair Ricky could not comprehend, but it made Priestly desperate, ugly. Anything, everything else, even what he'd said about his mother, Ricky could forgive. But not this. His small arm flashed out. He struck Priestly's face and fled into the darkness.

Priestly stood in the rain, the twenty pounds still in his hand. After a moment, he glanced down at the crumpled note as if he'd suddenly woken from a trance; and then he dropped it on the ground and wiped upon his soaking leg the fingers that had touched it.

27

THERE WAS HARDLY ROOM for them both in Sean's bunk bed.

"That was the most uncomfortable night I've ever spent," she said, her voice hoarse with sleep.

Sean looked into the dawning struggle of her face. He'd hardly slept because Caitlín had had no choice but to lie almost on top of him. None of it seemed quite real, her presence, their intimacy. Close to morning, he'd drifted off, but had been shocked out of sleep: the nightmare, too quickly evaporating, had been about his wife and Pierce, the dream's sullying residue leaving a sense that she was really gone, gone forever, swallowed into the shadow of the boy.

He pushed his hand through Caitlín's hair and kissed her. But, remaining from the dream somehow, the boy was there, in her face, in the kiss itself.

Caitlín finally extricated her numb and cramped limbs and pulled on her robe. She told him she was going to get some coffee for them both and left.

He thought back to the hope of his youth. From where had come this need in him to be the perfect man, to work himself into the weave of history, a thick, a bright, a dominant thread — for what? He thought of his parents asleep in front of the blue light of the television, and him standing in the doorway as a child staring at them, their mouths unhinged like corpses. Switching off the television, he'd watched that balling fist of light, had experienced, contained, for a moment, as only a child can, Nothing, all the vastness of it. It broke in his head as all the stars themselves might have broken in the darkness of space, flowering out like the sudden gape of a striking snake. What then? Then language, to begin the narrative of his life, for he had a susceptibility for language, for its power to appear to make things substantial, as if the secret of that first darkness were held in books, in the consecrating odor of old print and paper.

Senseless thoughts, senseless. Sean turned himself over and attempted to get comfortable in the tiny bunk. He was lost, trying to find the thread again. What had been wrong? Was it that he'd wished to be perfect, wished never to be evacuated, as so many are, by a television, sprawled, incontinent and unhinged, wished never to die by such increments. To be perfect. Which meant to be always alive. And this perhaps would have been possible if he'd not also been constitutionally condemned to *feel* profoundly, which brings with it a sympathy for the morbid. Will to perfection, depth of feeling — who could have withstood the tension of such inimical things so closely bound? Certainly he'd not withstood it long.

But perhaps there had never been a need to. Couldn't perfection have existed even more resonantly in the secret knowledge of its compromise? Couldn't the boy, if Sean had never sought him out, have been the third dimension of his text, hinted at but never clearly articulated, the shifted curtain, the vague shadow in the upper window of an ancient family home? Couldn't both their lives have ended without it ever being known that one had broken off into the other, that he'd jettisoned some part of himself into the underworld, the boy, his dark root, remaining in the soul of poverty, vice, aberration, alienation? Was such not the root of all perfection? But these were idle words, idle abstractions. He'd had two choices: to turn his back on or to accept this son. The consequences of both were terrible, the first spiritually, the second materially. But they were consequences for *him*. To do neither, to hold the boy in limbo as he had — *that* had been the sin.

"Christ," he said it softly into the air, and then over and over, "Christ, Christ, Christ," until Caitlín returned with two cups of coffee and lay back down beside him.

"I still can't believe she's dead," Caitlín said.

"Who?"

"Who do you think?"

"Oh, you mean Ronan's mother."

"Well has someone else died in the meantime?"

"She was so sick."

"She was as sick as she wanted to be; and she hadn't done with him yet."

"With Ronan?"

"Yes. It's funny. When you passed her door, you could

165

feel her. I mean I hardly ever actually saw or even heard her, but she was, for the most part, the dominant force of life in the home. I wrote about it in my little journal — I have a little journal, you know," she said bashfully, biting gently at the skin on his shoulder. "I have no sort of *percussive* life myself." She seemed uncomfortable with her words. "I feel like I'm just a kind of membrane, resonating with all the lives around me."

"Did you write that in your journal?"

"Yes," she said, with an ironic innocence. "How could you tell? Am I not normally this fluent?" Still she nuzzled into his shoulder, looking up at him at once coyly and brazenly. "But you could feel her. And you know the only presence stronger than hers was Devon's. But his was sort of inside you, whereas hers — "

"Beat its tattoo," he took up with mock grandiloquence, "upon your taut and responsive membrane, perhaps?"

"All right, all right," she said, frowning. "I won't quote from my journal again."

"No, no," he said apologetically, drawing her closer. "I'm only joking. Tell me, what do you mean you can't believe she's dead?"

She sighed, gathering her thoughts, then began very slowly. "I mean that what I feel . . ." She thought again for a moment. "What I feel in the house now is . . . amazement — *her* amazement. Maybe it's just because I caught a glimpse of her face when the ambulance came. It was amazed, it seemed to me, not even angry at the end. Do you know what it made me think of? It made me think of someone who puts on a particular personality, perhaps just as a game at first or to cover some weakness, for whatever reason, and then sort of forgets it, forgets that they're doing it. What she was amazed at was that the world had taken her — even in death, I mean — at face value, had taken her for that made-up self she'd long since forgotten she was wearing."

Sean considered this for a moment and then said, "What did you mean then that she hadn't finished with him?"

"I don't know. I think she had forgiven him, but perhaps she just didn't have enough resources left to express that forgiveness. It was like a concept that exists only in another culture: she simply didn't have the language for it."

"Forgiveness for what?"

"Haven't I told you about this?" She seemed surprised. "Well, there was this scandal that forced him to leave his church. Theresa talked to me about it one time. Nothing was ever proved and apparently the testimony of a number of the women was shown to be grossly inconsistent. I mean I'm sure his solicitations may have gone a little too far in some instances — I've often felt a bit uncomfortable with him myself. It's this sort of overbearing, paternal sympathy he seems to want to have for you. There's something creepy about it. I remember one time he pointed out a ladder in my tights, and it was almost as if he was going to cry, as if he wanted to attach all the sadness of my pathetic life to it. But I can't really believe that he was in any way calculating or malign — just weak. Just a little weak, like all of us. He's been so good to his mother, and she's never given him so much as a word of thanks. Not to mention how good he's been to all those boys and how much he truly, genuinely worries and cares about them. And how hard he works for them — he borrows money and puts his own savings into that home."

"And Theresa — was she a nun? She looks like a nun."

"Yes. She joined a strict order when she was very young, but she told me that one day she realized that she needed to find God in more than prayer and abstinence. She said that what finally convinced her that she had to leave was that one time, when she was repainting her little room in the nunnery, she had to take her crucifix off the wall, and as she did she almost dropped it. Just for a second, she told me, it slipped out of her hands before she caught it again. It was just indescribable, she said, the sheer intensity of her terror. She said her bowels had felt literally as if they'd turned to ice."

"How pleasant," Sean said, taking up Caitlín's hand and bringing it to his lips.

She pulled it away, obviously annoyed at his dryness.

"I don't really see the crisis," he said in his own defense, though also a little contritely. "It doesn't seem unnatural that a nun should feel that way about her crucifix."

"But the crucifix was made of tempered steel," she said with frustration, as if he were being deliberately obtuse. "If anything it would have just gouged a hole in the floor — "

"Yes, but — "

"*Listen.* In that fraction of a second just before she

caught it again, she'd seen it, had *felt* it shattering. And she told me that it was then that she'd realized just how fragile her God had become. Sean, what makes something strong is its flexibility. There was no liquid left in her God. That crucifix felt as if it had the brittleness of old bones."

"Your journal?" he playfully enquired.

"My journal," she admitted, without apology.

He stroked her hair away from her face. They smiled at each other. That's what she was, he thought, his liquid.

As he continued absently to stroke her hair, she frowned slightly.

"You see, last night," she said, as if everything else had just been a preface or a means to this, "I could feel you, but when it was over you were gone so quickly. I mean you weren't untender. You didn't just fall off and go to sleep, but you *were* gone, and so completely gone."

"I'm sorry," Sean said, his hand stilling upon her face, a fear rising instantaneously in his heart, a fear of *this* kind of intimacy.

"No, I didn't mean you to be sorry, I just . . ." She faltered, obviously annoyed at herself. "Anyway . . . anyway, I can't say it without you misunderstanding me."

He didn't say anything. It was a blow, like a blow with the flat of a hand upon the lungs, one that resonates throughout the body.

"Oh, why did I say that?" she asked herself, closing her eyes. "Why did I say that?"

She pulled herself suddenly up off the bed.

"I've got to go to work," she said.

Checking his alarm clock, she let out a shocked exclamation.

"Oh my God, I have ten minutes."

She bent back over the bed and kissed him, a firm kiss, too full of regret to be sensual, her eyes wide open.

28

WHEN SHE ENTERED her cabin to get changed for work, Caitlín stepped on an envelope that had obviously been pushed under her door the previous night. She picked it up and opened it.

Dear Miss Calhoun:

I understand that it's never fair to put someone unwillingly into a position of trust, but my hope is, nevertheless, that I can trust you. As you know, Sean — Mr. Hennessy — is looking for me. My guess is that he's being rather obscure about his reasons for this. As I'm sure he's told you, I was his foster son for a number of years. We were very close. We went through two tragedies together — the death of his son and the suicide of his daughter. To Liam and Megan I felt as close, I imagine, as I would feel to a real brother and sister. But these deaths, one following hard upon another, caused Sean, I believe, to suffer a kind of nervous breakdown. Ironically, if he'd been an ordinarily constituted, even a weak man, this would have run its course and he would, as much as one can after such things happen, have returned to some kind of normality. But the curse of his life then was that he was so strong — or desired (for reasons of his own) to be strong. I think he had no conception of the depth of his grief, and could not believe that anything could hurt him so profoundly. So, with all his strength, he determined to disperse this grief — and succeeded, dispersing it so thoroughly throughout himself that it could no longer be isolated and cut away, but became integral, transforming from a disorder of the nerves into the deepest and most frightening kind of madness. Those closest to him witnessed this and tried to make him see it. But he believed too much in his own strength. Finally, his wife could not take any more and left him. This, of course, made things even worse. And it was then that the idea entered his head that I had something to do with all these terrible events. It was the simplest of conclusions. After all, his family had been intact before my arrival — though the completely balanced mind would have taken into account Liam's chronic sickness and Megan's clinical depression, two things Sean had always had a tendency to deny.

So now he's looking for me, and I'm afraid to what end. You have to understand that I love him very much, that I love him as the person as close to a father as I can imagine. He was kind to me, and kind to take me in. Despite everything, those years that I spent with him and his family were the most "real" of my life; they anchored me and gave me some sense of substance — if only a single stitch to tie me to the weave of this world.

Miss Calhoun, I've been given to understand that you and he may be friends, and I have my own reasons to suspect that by now you may be more than friends — there's a certain intuition I've always had for fate.

Anyway, let me try to be more clear. I'm aware that he's looking for me. I knew it would happen because I know him

so well. I have a sense that, clutching to his seminal idea of
strength, he's trying to purge himself of that by now almost
constitutional madness. Through me. You will have to admit yourself that there is something obsessive in his search
for me. And I am, to say the least, frightened and worried, as
much for him as for myself. Of course, I could go to the
police or to social services, but there are a number of reasons why these options are not viable. In simple terms I'm
a homeless male prostitute making accusations about one
of the senior managers in the Birmingham social services.
There are also certain even more compelling reasons why it
would not be good for me right now to walk into a police
station. And I can't imagine, knowing Sean, that he appears
to be in an unreasonable state of mind.

But these are all by the by. The fact is that, as I've said
before, I still care about him very much — this is a ridiculous understatement. I love him as much as I've ever loved
anyone in my life. There is not an hour that goes by without
me thinking about him in one way or another. I feel that if
you and he are having a relationship, he's going some way
toward recovery. Perhaps you may find a way into him. This
is a great deal to ask of you, I know, and I have put myself
completely into your hands. But if you are invested enough
in Sean to not simply throw this letter away, I beg of you to
come and meet me tonight in the place where I'm staying so
that I may tell you everything and talk to you about how I
think this can be resolved. There is also something else that
I've not talked about, something that I could not commit to
paper for fear — well, you shall see. I'm staying now, hiding
I suppose, in an old site unit in an abandoned quarry near
Whittam Forest. It's a place I knew when I was living with
Sean. His old house is just a mile or so away; Sean's daughter
and I, and his son when he was well enough, used often to

play in and around this quarry and a few times secretly camped out in this old site unit. Now I've made it a sort of resort retreat when I want to get away from my various town residences.

I admit that I ask you to come here for my own safety. There are certain vantage points from which I can watch to see that you're approaching the site unit on your own. Forgive this please. After the life I've led, it's so difficult for me ever to trust anyone. You cannot imagine how hard it is even for me to write this to you, Miss Calhoun. I do not ask you to walk very far, though some of it is over pretty rough terrain when going down into the quarry itself; but as you will see with the map I've given you, there's a road called Drewers Lane just off the M6 down which you can drive almost all the way to the quarry. As I say, I have to be cautious. Make yourself at home in the cabin, and I shall meet you there at exactly eight o'clock.

Caitlín glanced over the map. She got off work at five today; it would take her perhaps two and a half hours to get there. She would have to leave straight from the home. Quickly she washed and made herself up, but as she was about to leave her cabin, she got a strange feeling in her lungs, as if they were distended like sails, fully rigged, dangerously rigged, in a high wind. Late as she was, she made herself sit down for a moment. She brought her hands together as in prayer and pressed them to her lips. Why had she slept with him? Why had she allowed herself to care for him? What was she to do with all of this? She checked her watch: no time to think. Thrusting the letter and the map into her satchel, she slipped out into the hallway. But just as she locked her door, Sean came out of his room in his robe to go to the shower. Glancing nervously at him, she smiled but felt a touch of fear, not knowing what really lay behind that strong Irish face.

"Are you going to make it?" he asked, intensifying his gaze, having noticed, with the sensitivity of a new lover, her discomfort, the dishonest flicker of her eyes.

"I hope so," she said, kissing him quickly as she passed.

29

SEAN WAS TROUBLED by that meeting with Caitlín in the hall. That flicker of her eyes, that nervously cast smile had, just for a second, made him feel again the full extent of what he'd lost. How was it that he'd managed to *keep* hold of nothing? Was this not even part of his need to find the boy — that the boy was, in a way, all that he had left?

For want of a better idea, he decided to drive into the city, just to drive around, looking, hoping, as one might search for someone one cannot believe is dead, feeling that stab each time a stranger passes wearing their features, using their gestures, speaking in their voice. It was as if he were going out to seek the soul of his past, a soul now shattered and scattered like the last sunlight upon the Thames.

Sean left the boat.

As he put the key into his car door, a small, cautious voice called to him.

"Oi, mista, mista."

Sean turned around. On the other side of the towpath, half hidden beneath an ailanthus, stood that little boy he'd picked up in his car one time. As Sean approached, the boy's almost parodic circumspection infected him, and he glanced uneasily around.

"You told me free 'undred if I 'elp you find Priestly."

"You know where he is?"

The boy seemed changed. The sores beneath his nose were now disguised with foundation; his eyes, large in his thin face, bespoke a desperation that had almost superseded that former innocence; and he kept spitting, as if there were some bitterness in his mouth.

"Four 'undred," the boy said. "I'll tell you for four 'undred."

Sean stepped a little closer and looked down at this sickly boy in his filthy cardigan. Christ, he looked like an old man.

"Where is he then?" Sean said.

"I know where you live," the boy said. It was a threat.

Sean almost smiled. "I'll give you the money."

"You betta, 'cos I know where you live," the boy repeated.

Sean waited while this boy, with his oversized head, his underdeveloped body cassocked in that old cardigan, struggled to look tough.

"Don't tell 'im who told ya."

"I won't."

"'E's only go'n' a be there tonight. 'E's stayin in this derilic' brewery down by the river. You know where 'ammersmif bridge is?"

"I know where you mean."

"Yeah, it's just down from there, beside this — "

"I know," Sean cut the boy off. "I know exactly where you mean."

For a moment the boy tried again to conjure a tough look, and then, as he started to walk away, repeated his threat, "I know where you live."

"Wait a minute," Sean called to him. "Wait here."

The boy looked frightened suddenly. Sean went quickly to his cabin and took four hundred from where he kept his cash, returned, and handed it to the boy.

Holding the money, the boy seemed perplexed, abashed, his innocence flooding back, dissolving all the hard lines of his experience. It was as if he didn't want it, hadn't expected it, as if he'd thought of this merely as some make-believe. Now these notes in his hand told him it was real.

For a moment Sean actually thought the boy was going to give the money back, his meager face blasted with innocence.

"F — fanks," the boy stammered finally, jamming the notes roughly into the pocket of his cardigan as he turned and began to move quickly away, and then to trot, and then to run, forgetting about the money, all the future it promised, the sun, the ocean, beauty and immortality. By the black mud of the Thames he ran.

30

THERESA WALKED WEARILY UP THE STAIRS, pausing for a moment at the door of the room that had been her mother-in-law's. She put her hand upon it, felt still the life it had once contained.

At last the home was empty. Two new placements from the university had taken the boys out to a movie. Caitlín, who'd seemed extremely distracted today, had left at exactly five. And Ronan had gone to his mother's grave to plant roses. A sickness of remorse had seemed to descend upon him since his mother's death, making the distance between Theresa and her husband even vaster than before. She thought of that incident yesterday, where she'd begun to climb the stairs just at the moment he'd come out of his room to descend. Catching sight of each other, they'd both instinctively faltered, and finally he'd turned around, frowning to affect forgetfulness, and had reentered his room. She knew it was the fear in them both of that moment they would have passed each other on the stairs, passed *through* each other, like ghosts sharing the same home but different worlds of grief.

She entered her room, switched on the single dim lamp beside her bed, and genuflected before her crucifix. Only six o'clock and pitch-dark. Could she stand another winter? And then how many more without him, for she felt that he was never returning? And in a few years he could not return — not dead, but a man, which was the same. A man? She tried but could not conceive of him beyond a face still wet with light.

Stealthily Theresa locked her door, as if fearing to wake the house itself. She went over to her cupboard, reached up, and removed from behind its ornate wooden pediment a large black cash box. After opening this and placing it on the floor, she undressed and knelt before it, this pious woman, gaunt almost to emaciation, the bones of her naked body etched in her skin. From the box, across which her shadow fell, she now removed his T-shirt and slipped it on. As she made her way back to her bed a tremor ran through her spine. The T-shirt felt strangely cold. She placed her hands on the front of the T-shirt and looking down at them saw that they were stained with fresh blood. A strangled cry escaped her, both fearful and ecstatic. His dried blood had somehow liquefied; it was all over the T-shirt and her hands. She looked up at her crucifix and her legs went hollow. Almost collapsing, she hissed out, "Mother of God." The crucifix was gone.

"Would you mind very much if I borrowed Him?"

In terror, she reeled around, falling onto the bed, banging her back against the headboard. Devon sat in her reading chair, cradling the crucifix in his arms, his hands dark with blood.

"I just wondered if you wouldn't mind terribly? Just for tonight." His tone was flat, detached, but his eyes, fixed upon her, were filled with a wild despair. And something else. Hatred.

Pulling herself up, she knelt on the bed facing him. She couldn't have approached any closer, not with his eyes bearing upon her in that way.

"Your hands are bleeding," she said, trying to keep calm.

"Don't wet your knickers. They're bleeding because I cut them." He revealed in his hands a jagged fragment of brown glass. "With this, in fact." An unnatural smile broke up through his lips, as if with the subterranean pressure of that hateful euphoria. "It's from a bottle of Woodpeckers."

"Why?" she said quietly, feeling her heartbeat in her throat.

"Because it's sweet and appeals to the half of me that's still a child."

"I mean why did you cut yourself?" she quietly persisted.

To this he gave no answer.

"Why are you staring at me like that?" she said, her voice becoming hoarse.

He went to speak but suddenly blanched and seemed in too much pain. He looked as if he were badly wounded, pale and doubled over, cradling the crucifix. But finally another unnatural smile broke at his lips.

"Because you hurt me," he said, looking up at her. "Because you have no density. Because you give me no place to rest." He spoke with barely stifled viciousness and a terrifying conviction.

"I would have offered you anything," she retorted.

"But you *have* nothing," he said with vehemence. "You *are* nothing. And because you love me, I have to live in that." Frowning, he looked off into the darkness, anxious, as if he'd sensed something, someone perhaps in the house, or even hidden in the shadowed recesses of the room.

He remained quiet for a while, staring, listening. He looked hunted, haunted, and she kept completely still, balanced, unbreathing, upon his precariousness.

At last, he turned back to her, his face suddenly completely untroubled. In a matter-of-fact tone, he said, "Do you know that old man, the one the kids call Eggy because he smells so bad? Tall, thin man, has a sort of swelling on his neck, always wears a trilby and a suit that's become glossy with grease? You can see him around here all the time. He's been banned from every pub. He's always raging at invisible tormentors."

She nodded.

"Well, do you know how he got banned from the Queen's Arms?"

"No."

"It was the last pub that would have him, poor bugger. But apparently one day he was sitting on a stool at the bar, and suddenly he stood up, rigid as a sergeant major. The barman told me that there was this odd look in Eggy's face, a kind of frowning, twitching look of extreme concentration. He thought that he was about to begin one of his tirades — either that or was having some kind of minor stroke. But then Eggy delicately pinched up the cloth at the left knee of his trousers and shook it. And out of the hem slipped a single firm turd, which Eggy then picked up and placed, as if it were a cigar, into the ashtray."

The boy made a grotesque attempt at laughter. After this his head sunk, and Theresa thought, for a moment, of approaching him. But a second later he was staring at her again, somewhat composed, though his eyes were once more filled with that angry, euphoric intensity.

"It's probably an apocryphal story," he said. "But he deserves it. And those who deserve an apocrypha, well, I find a peace in them. Even in the men who fuck me, I find peace, in all the lies of their lives, because they're only living when they can hold a smooth blushed cheek against a blackness in their loins, and then they return to their fat wives. I love them. You can't ever know what peace, what hope they give me. But *you* . . ." And now a tremor, querulous, despairing, and incredulous in his voice, "I can't find peace in you —

"Mrs. Twinkle," he broke off abruptly. "Have you ever heard of Mrs. Twinkle? You might have read about her. Some years ago it was in all the papers. I knew her. She lived in the council estate where my mother and I lived. Sometimes she'd throw buckets of water over us kids from her balcony; and sometimes she'd give us sweets. And the sweets were often wet — *really* wet — though we ate them anyway. Until I realized that her dog. I think it was a cross between a pug and a pitbull, the ugliest looking creature you've ever seen, with two pointed ears and this enormous heavy black tongue, always hanging out. Anyway, until I realized that they were wet because her dog had been licking them. And do you know what she did? It was in all the papers for a while. She poisoned four children. Quite methodically. She bought lemon sherbets, carefully gutted them of all their original sherbet, mixed the sherbet with some kind of rat poison and then refilled the sweets. When the police finally broke into her flat, she had the dead kids all propped up in chairs around her dinner table. She'd dressed them all in these period costumes she'd made, as if they were Victorian dolls, like a little Merchant Ivory production. She was in a costume herself, and they were having high tea. One of the policemen told me that it was such an unreal scene — the four dead kids slumped in the chairs, and her talking sweetly and offering them French Fancies. But the strangest thing, he said, was the dog, which was sitting at the other end of the table, opposite her, its hind legs on a chair, its forelegs on the table. He said it was just as if he were looking at a demon, a real demon, with those hornlike ears, blinking its eyes like a great toad, that huge black tongue draped from its mouth. He didn't tell the newspapers this, of course, but he told me. I was just a boy. He was one of my mother's many lovers. He told me — he was very troubled and needed to tell someone who wouldn't have him certified — that he knew that it all came down somehow to the dog, that the dog had conceived this, that the dog was the Devil himself . . . and this . . ." The boy frowned, seemed a little confused, but then said with redoubled intensity, "*this is true* . . . Mrs. Twinkle." And then with equal confusion and intensity: "It's not *true*. It's not true, but it's more true than you are. And you might ask me

why I ever came to you in the first place. Well, I was fascinated with you, I was fascinated that an emptiness so complete that it would seem to need a vastness to express it
could be so skillfully, so . . . *economically* contained; I-I-I"
(he was breathless, stammering, his eyes wild) "was drawn
to you because I did not *believe* you, pushed out of your
nest, you germ of flight in your shattered shell, grotesque,
doomed. That's what you are: fascinating in the most grotesque way, life trembling and translucent, nerves in aspic.
But I can't enter you. You offer nothing, no chance of life in
yourself." He seemed to be trying to remember something.
"What was that? Where was it I saw that? What am I
thinking of? I can't remember. I-I-I *can't* remember." And
suddenly back to her. "You offer nothing, have nothing,
you feed from a man who was nailed to his wings. I am a
fake!" he suddenly shouted, showing her his cut hands.
"But it's you who makes me a fake, because you believe in
all my sins, because if you could you'd wear them about
your bones, you'd take them from this world into the next,
you'd take them to heaven and feed them to the angels —
as if the angels were pigeons, I were stale bread, and you
were mad with loneliness. Christ, Christ, Christ — " It
was just the word, voluptuously exhaled, not a name, not
a supplication, just a form of sound. "You make it so easy
for me to be a fake. I took that crucifix right off the wall
as you were staring at your bloody hands." Abruptly he
stood, letting the crucifix fall to the floor. "What am I
meant to *do?*" he shouted at her. "What am I meant to do
to forgive you?"

"I've never asked anything of you," she said, trying to push her voice to more than a hoarse whisper.

"No, you haven't. That's right," he said, suddenly calming, returning to himself, that contained smile vividly reasserting his beauty. "No, you've never asked or expected anything. You're a good woman, Theresa." His tone was now almost sensual, and ominous as he sat down on the bed before her. She was still kneeling, and he'd sat very close, his face just an inch or so from hers. Her heartbeat thundered in her chest, her throat, her head, as she lifted her hand to his face, touched it. But as she moved it away, she left a smear of his own blood over his cheek, remembered the blood on his, on her hands, remembered that she was naked but for his small, torn T-shirt. Impulsively reaching down, she tugged at the hem to cover her bare legs, and then looked up into his face again.

Something she recognized, knew too well, glimmered in his eyes.

"My sister," he said, "you think I'd fuck you, you bag of bones." Suddenly, with one powerful hand, he took hold of her chin and thrust her down on the bed. He pinned her with his body, his hand clamping her jaw. She felt that at a whim he could snap her neck. He brought his face right down to hers. "Sister, you're grotesque," he said into her face, his breath smelling of smoke and decay, "and there's no one, nothing I've ever hated more in the world than you. You've never seen me, even once. You've never known my real name because you've never asked. All you saw in me was your redemption and that's what hurt me, because you never made yourself worth redeeming." Voluptuously, he paused. "But I'll give it to you anyway. " And forcing her mouth open with his superhuman hands, he pressed his lips, lips salty with the musk of men, to Theresa's, and breathed into her.

Then he was gone.

From her window he climbed down into the alley behind the home. He seemed hardly able to hold himself up, as if he were drunk or sick. Finally he collapsed beside a dustbin, shaking, his eyes wide, maniacal, like a man just coming out of a seizure, his mouth wet and trembling, small convulsions twitching his body. He entered a sleep as absolute as death. But only briefly, just until he became slack, expressionless again. Tabula rasa, the breathless, moonlacquered lake of childhood. A moment later his eyes opened, and with a will and physical strength of which only he was capable, he dragged himself to his feet and slouched off in the cold darkness toward the river.

31

July 12th

THIS SHALL BE MY LAST ENTRY. Strange to think it, this voice on the white page, my voice in ink and the motion of my hand, to be heard by your eyes. Dad. Understand. You need to fall. To be broken. What I'm most sorry about is that you've not known Durward, not known his name and who he is, that he's a way into the infinite, that he can, with his words, make me see everything. Momentarily. You have to understand then — and it was my choice, <u>my</u> choice — that the cost of this is that you cannot bear the prosaic, the hum of the milkvan, the morning light through the windows, clock-radios. All those things, Dad, from which you're made. Do you sleep? Dad, do you sleep? You gave your soul no place inside you, so it returned to you in us, Liam and me, a silent clamor of sunlight reflected up from the ocean upon your bronze limbs. You have to understand that at one end there is the infinite, Durward's voice in the darkness and the way we exchange our bodies, our lives, the way he strips me of every construct. And at the other, your feet and your hands, powerful, veined and callused, like a fossil of sensuality, like the love of men for bones. That's what this world wishes me to find a way to worship, those hands and those feet, to swell my breasts, to strip my hair of darkness and live in the giddy stupor of being wanted. Now Liam has returned to us, is in my belly growing, our child. So we are ready. I'm not afraid. My last entry. Strange. How strong my voice seems. I look back at it, this thing I've made, the words on the page. And it's impossible. To create is to do the impossible. But we've forgotten this. Just everywhere those massive hands and feet, the power of pure inertia.

Dad, I'm sorry for what pain this will cause you, but understand that for Durward and me there is — there <u>was</u> no choice.

32

THE LAST SUNLIGHT reflected up from the Thames and through the smashed windows at the very top of the brewery to swarm upon the ceiling. Here and there still, remnants of the yellow ribbons of the police cordon. Her naked body lay beneath a piece of blue tarpaulin. The forensic evidence showed that she'd suffered terribly before she'd died. She evoked the kind of desire that was a corruption, but was herself a complete and rogue innocence, an innocence over which one could have no control, like the movement of sunlight upon this ceiling. The man who'd done it was, so to speak, a very ordinary man, for whom his desire and her innocence had become a way into the inconceivable. A colorless man. The conductor of the bus one catches to work, whom you secretly dub "Moonface." Your colleague, the thin man with the goatee, who always seems a little abstracted and still lives with his mother. At a party one time, he got drunk on piña coladas and did push-ups on the floor with a rose between his teeth; at home he lies curled beneath his bed sheets, flooding his mind with Mahler from his headphones and eating piles of tangerines. A docent at the National Gallery who talks to herds of bored schoolchildren about *The Execution of Lady Jane Grey: Why do you think her blindfold is white? Why do you think it seems like a stage? Why is the executioner so epicene and provocative?* One's own brother, who drinks a little too much and makes jokes even about the discovery that he's dying of cancer — *Christ, can you never be serious about anything?* Men. All men. What was found, what was uncovered here was their hopeless humor. But where was the violence? Where were those actual moments, which must have echoed out against these walls, impacting inward, blows of sound? We can never get to that place. It was back in our dream time, for she has been here, naked under that piece of tarpaulin in a defunct brewery forever. So what does it mean that men have found her now, have buried her with the consecration of a dead religion among the prosaic dead, among the dead dead? Have emptied this place of her (which they can never do) and have cried out that the fears in our dreams have found incarnation, that there is a monster loose among us?

33

SEAN GOT INTO THE BREWERY by one of the boarded windows that had already been pushed in — pushed in by him, in fact, those years and years ago when he'd come to this place. He entered stealthily, hoping that the boy had not yet arrived so that he could have time to prepare himself.

He felt nauseous, each throb of his heart threatening to break it from its moorings. He passed through a labyrinth of rusting cylindrical vats brooding massively in the darkness and finally entered that room on the river side of the brewery in which her body had been found. The moon was almost full, flooding into those shattered, unboarded windows a good sixty feet above him. He remembered everything, the forest of square columns, the glass that snapped and crunched beneath his feet, that small alcove in the corner where her body had been found beneath a piece of blue tarpaulin. But somehow he'd remembered the room as much larger, as if it were a strange room he'd entered in childhood, which had been absorbed into his soul as a space for the forbidden.

Near the alcove were the remains of a fire beside which lay an old sleeping bag. He hunkered beside the nest of ashes, putting down the iron bar and the rope he'd brought with him. He'd wrenched the bar from the broken cast-iron fence of a derelict house, and it still bore its spearhead finial. Leaning down further, Sean lifted the mouth of the sleeping bag and inhaled its odor. He flinched with the shock of it. Revolting. For some reason he'd expected to smell the boy as he'd smelled him as a child fresh from a bath.

Beside the sleeping bag lay a green kit bag, such as sailors carry. Sean undid the tie, but the moment he pulled it open he screamed and fell backward. It was a head. He'd seen a human head. After briefly gathering himself, he took up the iron bar, widened the mouth of the kit bag, and poked gingerly at that profusion of blond hair. His body slackened and he released a sigh of relief as he fished out the wig and held it suspended before him.

Casting the wig aside, he searched through the bag, which reeked of stale underwear, of sweat and cloying commingled perfume and cologne, a compost of clothes. Inside were a number of wigs, shoes, and garments, both male and female, each one of which he lifted to his face to smell, flinching every time. He found nothing not imbued with that vile marriage of scents. There were photographs scattered randomly among the clothes: the boy with various families that had fostered him; with Sean and his family;

with Ronan and Theresa and the other children at the home; with some of the rent-boys Sean had picked up in his car at Victoria — one picture of them all feasting in a filthy alleyway, that little boy who'd come to his boat last night looking almost unrecognizably happy among them. And there was also a recent picture of the boy with a very over-weight and unhealthy looking man. They were both sitting in a booth at an Indian restaurant, the boy feeding the man, the man laughing, curry sauce drooling down his chin. Sean noticed that the man wore two watches on one wrist. Right at the bottom of the bag, jutting from the pocket of a pair of tiny cutoff jeans, he found a picture of Sandra, the boy's mother, lovely, but empty, abysmal, as if the camera had caught her just at the moment between selves, her face like a clay mask, a form into which life had not yet been breathed. The cutoffs, Sean then realized, were the ones the boy had been wearing when Sean had seen him in the street, thinking he was a woman, attracted by his legs. These too he brought to his nose, but this time the smell was so vile he began to gag, and finally spat into the darkness.

Quickly he shoved everything back, and it was just as he pulled the drawstring closed that he noticed it, dark and with an oily sheen. Lifting a corner of the sleeping bag, he revealed it more fully. A sheet of blue tarpaulin.

"Dad!"

Sean wheeled round, the percussion of it in the bones of his head, echoing around this small vast room. Then it was gone, completely gone, just silence. But he'd heard it, some-one crying out "Dad." Crouching, clutching his steel bar he

listened for the boy. But nothing. Had it come from a child
on the towpath or on a passing boat? But he could hear no
footsteps on the loose stones, no engine. Was it an animal
sound, a bird of some kind? But it had seemed so distinct,
that "Dad" cried into the air, cried at him. And he'd reso-
nated with it because he'd known it, knew it still. It was
exactly the "Dad" of the first and only time the boy had
ever called him "Dad," that "Dad" half caught in the air, as
if the boy had wanted to swallow it back again. Sean had
been tickling them both, Megan and the boy, leaning into
the back of the car from the driver's seat while his wife was
reading the map and telling him rather bad-temperedly to
stop getting them into a state. But they were both crimson-
faced with laughter; he'd brought them to bloom. He remembered the great joyous bubble of snot swelling from his
daughter's nose as she screamed for him to stop, hardly able
to breathe with her laughter. Then he'd start on the boy,
who was looking at his half-sister's unrestrained happiness
as if trying to comprehend it, to get it inside himself. Then
he'd look wildly at Sean, with that smile of his that was
beyond laughter, as if trying to understand that this was
a kind of happiness. Though the boy didn't laugh himself, he squirmed and manifested that smile that was a
laughter too abandoned to express, that was joy forgotten
in joy. Like Megan, the boy got to the point where he could
hardly breathe — hardly breathe — and it was then, suddenly, that the boy had cried out, "Dad!" Sean had frozen
as if the boy had struck his face, had then quietly turned
back around to his irritated wife, who was still searching

the map for where they were and where they were meant to be going, that "Dad" like a dying bird, grounded, fluttering hopelessly. Now, leaning before the boy's wretched sleeping bag, his fetid sack of clothes, Sean pressed his hands to his eyes. Why had he turned his back? Why had he started the car and begun to drive, his wife telling him not to, that they'd only get more lost? But he'd continued driving. Sean now uncovered his eyes and picked up the rope, and as he did so it occurred to him that he hadn't remembered Liam. His son must have been in the back of the car also, but Sean couldn't picture him at all, though he recalled Megan and the boy vividly. His sick son who he could not dare to bring to such a state of euphoria. He'd conflated them, the boy and his son, for, in a way, weren't they just alike? — his son experiencing his joy vicariously and the boy trying to learn happiness from the outside in, trying to plunge, to quench the form of happiness in his heart. The only real laughter, the only feeling not coveted, stolen, counterfeited, fed from, was that of his daughter. Who the boy had killed. The boy had killed her. And had killed his son, and — he was now convinced of it — had somehow sent his wife reeling off, as good as dead to him. So vividly again, Sean could see, could feel, the boy squirming under his tickling fingers, that unnatural smile — demonic. The boy had destroyed his life. And again, like the fresh convulsions of a sickness he'd hoped had passed, it came flooding in, that blinding, incandescent fury which turned everything ashen.

In the darkness now, he squatted behind one of the concrete pillars close to the boy's things, clutching his weapon and his rope, and waited.

The map he'd given her was flawless. The road had brought her right to the edge of the quarry. Caitlín climbed her way down in the half darkness toward the light of that small site building. As she approached, she could hear the hum of a petrol generator, and realizing that he must have switched it on, wondered, looking around the dark precipices, from where he was watching her. Nervously, she knocked before entering.

Inside, there was a single cot bed covered in army surplus blankets. Beside it, on an upturned milk crate, sat a cassette-clock-radio, an old one in which the numbers rotated into place with a sudden hum and click. On the floor lay, as if taken off in a hurry, an old pair of monkey boots, a pair she could remember the boy wearing, and which now made him strangely present. The numbers on the clock read 19:15. She stared at it until the clock began to hum. The 5 trembled and the minutes rotated: 19:16. She sat herself on the bed and waited.

The fatman pulled his van off the road and drove it down a rough gravel path to the edge of a small lake. Things, so far, had been more or less as the boy had said, though it had taken him over two and a half hours to get here, not the two the boy had estimated. The fatman checked all three of his watches as well as the nurse's breast watch. It was only just gone seven now, and the boy had assured him that it would take less than half an hour to get from this lake to the quarry. Everything else was just as the boy had said it would be. The van was now hidden from the road, and the fatman could see at the far end of the lake that path that led off into the woods. This, according to the detailed map the boy had drawn him, led over one hill and down into the quarry. With a thrill of panic, he checked the map again. In it the boy had given him all the estimated times between various landmarks as well as the latest times he could arrive at the landmarks and still make it to the site building before eight. The fatman had wanted to leave London much earlier, but the boy had got himself into an emotional state, and had needed comforting. Still, he had plenty of time.

Now, from the back of his van, he removed the pickax handle. It felt incredibly light, too light to kill. He'd had dreams last night that she wouldn't die, that no matter how hard he beat her, she would keep getting up and crawling away from him, the bloody pulp of her crawling like an insect. She was not human — not human. For the last few days the boy had hardly let him sleep, but had revealed to him all of the obscenely cruel things she'd done to him and to other children. And while telling him, the boy had kept him looking at the photograph of her face, had steeped each feature in evil, and had then shown him pictures of terrifying things, closeups of the heads of spiders and insects, of snakes and rats, and then again her face. The boy had told him that she liked to make tape recordings of the sufferings of those she tortured, to listen to the tape as she and that man coupled. . . . The fatman had been so tired and weak because he'd thrown up after almost every meal the boy had cooked for him. He didn't know why until the boy told him that it was her face. True enough, when he'd looked at the photograph the nausea had welled up in him again. Still now he could feel the foul dregs of it in his stomach. And in these last few days, when he could not take it anymore, the boy would soothe him, would sing to him, would tell him of their future together, after all of this, that they would both move to a place by the sea in Cornwall. But the pickax handle still seemed too light to kill that creature. Despite the cold night, sweat beaded on his forehead and his heart felt as if it were skipping, flipping, plunging, the beats like flat stones flung across a rough lake. Sleep, all the sleep he'd not had, like a fog now condensed in his limbs, in his head. He hardly knew how he'd driven here; it was as if he'd done it in a dream. He took the photograph from his pocket, her photograph, and looked down at her, those foul lees rising in him, that vile face. He could not look into it and flung the photograph into the back of his van, slamming the door shut with all his strength, as if upon the monster herself, and set off.

Sean became alert. He could hear footsteps on the loose gravel of the towpath. Slowly he rose from his crouched position, pressing his back against the pillar. Now the footsteps echoed on the concrete floor of the vat room. He felt dizzy, the knuckles of his trembling hands going white about the iron bar and rope, his body becoming rigid. Now the scrape and crunch of glass; and then it stopped. Sean brought himself to look around the column. The boy was squatting with his back to Sean, opening the kit bag. Just two strides away. Just two strides. Just two. Like a wave, fear itself lifted and hurled Sean upon the boy, who crumpled beneath his full weight. He wrenched the boy's arms up behind his back until he cried out with pain. Sean, remembering the boy's unnatural strength, had been ready for a brutal struggle, but even as he tied his wrists together the boy remained completely limp.

Picking up the iron bar, which he'd dropped while tying the boy's hands, he dragged the boy over to the alcove and shoved him down on one side of it while he sat against the other, recovering his breath. At last, face to face. The boy half sat, half lay helpless in an oddly flaccid, feminine way, his head tilted so that the top of it rested against the frame of one of the boarded-up windows, his dyed blond hair, now shoulder length, falling across his face, his bare legs, covered in cuts from the glass on the floor, bent at the knee and held tightly together as if Sean had also tied his ankles. The boy breathed with a sensual heaviness, like a captured heroine in an old movie. He was wearing a tiny pair of silvery shorts and a white blouse now speckled with blood; on his feet a pair of women's red, flat-soled shoes. Sean, also breathing hard, stared at the boy, who did not even look at him, but seemed entirely involved in his capture, in filling out its form, expressing it.

Finally, Sean spoke. "I had to tie you up, but I'm not going to hurt you."

"Said the vicar to the showgirl," the boy said, producing

that smile of his as he pulled his head up to look at Sean, his hair subsiding over it.

"Why are you staying *here?*" Sean asked. "Why *here?*"

"Because I was born here," the boy said flatly, his smile evaporating, his face hardening, shrinking back from that pose of wanton helplessness. "A child is born where his mother suffers most — is that not always true?" And then he tried to produce that smile again, though it seemed a little forced this time, and his voice was trying too hard to keep its smooth modulation. It caused Sean, just for a second, to wonder if this was the boy. Nothing was quite right: that voice, that strained smile, that almost burlesque pose, his feet bulging unattractively in those women's shoes.

But of course it was the boy.

"I need to know," Sean said, bringing himself back to his task. "I just need to know why you did it. I need to know. . . . I need to know, do you *feel* anything? Do you truly *feel* anything inside you?"

"Do you mean am I a monster?" the boy said softly. "And what if I said no? And what if I said yes? What if — "

"You *killed* my children." Sean's shout echoed metallically in the alcove. And then quietly, intensely: "They were innocent. Why would you kill them?"

The boy looked down into the floor, his face void of expression. "Your son died of an asthma attack; your daughter committed suicide as a result of clinical depression," he said as if he were repeating something he'd learned by rote. "And they were not innocent. I loved them both."

"Are . . . you . . . mad?" Sean said, a pause between each

drawn-out and desperate word. It was an honest, agonized appeal, which he repeated: "Are you mad?"

"I don't think so. I've always been too confused to be mad."

"You killed them. You killed them both. I have my daughter's diary."

"No, no, no, no, no, no," the boy said with pitying affection, looking up, "you have *my* diary." Now he continued with a cold, glib matter-of-factness. "I left it for you in her little desk. Not that it's not true. Essentially everything in it is true. She just did it so badly. Her own diary was typically teenage — maudlin, filled with 'profound' lines from popular songs, bits of her own dreadful poetry. And of course she left out a lot of the really good stuff, afraid in case you ever did get hold of it. She also talked about her depression, but it was such a commonplace depression; it was going nowhere; the truth is that she didn't really have a talent for it. The truth is," he paused, "that I could be a better she than she was." He paused again, thinking. "Sad. That's all you know of her, that diary. It's so sad. I'm sure you've pored over it a thousand times, perhaps even felt a melancholy glimmer of pride for her intelligence and articulateness, perhaps — "

Sean cut him off. "You did not write that diary. You did not write it. I know you didn't."

The boy waited a moment, as if Sean had merely been sneezing or clearing his throat, and then somewhat more somberly continued. "Of course the version of the diary I wrote for your wife was actually much harder to do. You see, I needed to convince your wife of something that was not empirically true — that you'd had a relationship with Megan that had somewhat broken the bounds of what's considered appropriate between father and daughter, and that her confusion over this had been the reason for her depression and suicide."

Sean sat trembling, staring at the boy who'd again paused for a moment.

"You see — "

He broke in, shaking, incredulous. "You made my wife believe I'd sexually abused my daughter?"

"Oh no, not anything so crude. If I'd done that she would have gone to the police or confronted you. It would all have been ruined. No, in that diary I created between you and Megan something full of nuance, the kind of subtle telepathic romance of any kind of forbidden longing. The language I used was that of illicit love, not abuse. And I think the way I played you in the diary was quite believable because I have imagined so many times that similar mistake of longing you made once before — "

"You knew — "

The boy cut him off. "And I knew your daughter well enough and loved you well enough to capture all her equivocal longing toward you. It was more true than the truth you got in the diary I had you find, which had been altered only in skill, style, and emphasis. If the pages of each one of those diaries were plucked, pressed, and fermented, the one your wife got would taste vividly, mnemonically, while the underlying insipidness of yours would numb the tongue. Oh yes, your wife's version was the truth under pressure, inspired, beautiful, while the diary you got required me only to pin a mane onto an ass. *An ass*. It was memoir — the commonplace done up like a dog's dinner. In your wife's I had to weave from all the events and incidents she would remember a web in which the lie would quiver helplessly, bringing the truth to life, sending it scuttling to feed upon the vitality of the lie. I had to calculate it very finely, to step out as far as I'd ever dared upon the thin ice of my instinct for people, for her — Rea. And my instinct was right. She did exactly what I half prayed, half expected her to do. She simply cut you off, cut you out of her life, which was a thing she was predisposed to do with all people who hurt her. I'd seen her do it before even with friends of long standing. I could feel it in her, that volatile tenderness that could never forget injury. It was her weakness, her flaw — that she would never confront, but would implacably withdraw. I know you felt it too, that predisposition in her — and that that, in fact, was one of the reasons for the intensity of your love for her, was why all men loved her, because you could feel her soul through her flesh, completely feminine, incommensurable, urging toward you or recoiling from you with equal ferocity."

"You're a liar," Sean shouted.

"You'll never know," the boy returned with equal force. "The fruit in the garden was not about knowledge, but about not knowing, about looking into a face and having no idea whether you should kiss it or strike it. Hell is a thousand such small abysses."

"That diary was written by my daughter. I know it was," Sean insisted.

"Does it frighten you to realize how little you knew her? Or is it more frightening that I am so effortlessly better at being your daughter than she ever was?"

"I *knew* my daughter — "

"I cut my finger this morning," the boy suddenly broke in in Megan's voice, all the expressions in his face exactly like hers, "chopping onions. The cut didn't bleed at first, as if it were amazed, like men in the movies when they're killed, powerful, evil men. Their eyes go wide because they're dead. And that was my finger with the cut in it. For a second, wide eyes, and then I pushed at the skin, the hero pulls out his sword, and it gaped. And then streams of blood; and I just couldn't stop looking at it, bleeding. And I wondered what would happen if I just kept letting it bleed. When would I know I was dead, when would it be too late — "

Sean shot forward, and using his fist like a hammer brought it down on the side of the boy's face. It was a blow in which he felt the bone of the boy's cheek resonate. At the impact the boy's head spun around, striking the frame of the boarded-up window beside him.

Slowly the boy turned his head back around to look at Sean. There was a cut just above his eyebrow from which blood streamed down his cheek. He looked almost serene, a smile ghosting his lips, his face expressing the soft baffled amazement of a person encountering something both inconceivable and inevitable.

Sean sat heavily back, staring at the boy, his whole body shaking.

To stop the blood from running into it, the boy closed his left eye, and after a moment asked, matter-of-factly, "What time is it?"

Caitlín checked the cassette-clock-radio: 19:40. She felt trapped in this place. An insidious, feral musk rose from the blankets on the bed. Hanging on the wall beside the door was the one decoration of the room, a framed photograph of Sean and the boy, the boy perhaps ten or eleven years old, clutching Sean's legs as if he were trying to bring him down with a rugby tackle, both faces replete with joy and exertion. Despite how small the cabin was, Caitlín kept turning around to look behind her, sure somehow that the boy would simply manifest himself in the cabin, like something precipitated from one's dreams, like the face your fears assume so that they can get close enough to kiss your throat. There was no sound but that of a faint wind, which gently rocked the cabin, and the periodic hum and click of the old cassette-clock-radio.

Seven-thirty-five, seven-forty-two, seven-thirty-seven, seven-forty-five. The fatman was frantic, staring at his watches beneath the torchlight before sending it stabbing again through the woods. He was walking and running alternately. It was so much further than the boy had said. Just ten minutes, he'd said, from the lake to the bottom of the hill. But now almost twenty-five minutes had passed, and the hill was just coming into sight. "Christ, Christ," the fatman kept muttering, not even a curse, not even conscious of it, his lungs like two heavy skins of liquid, sharp pains fissuring his ribs. The panic was all over him, like a fire he couldn't put out, snatching away his breath. If he didn't get to her in time, she would go; and when she found out that her mate had been killed, she would ship the boy to the police. He'd lost Feederboy; if he lost the boy, he would have lost everything. What else would he have to live for? Nothing. Nothing. And he was late, always late, like the boy said. He checked his watches again because all the energy and strength he had left in his body was in his panic. He drove himself on, shifting the pickax handle from hand to hand, for now it had found its weight, and hit the bottom of the hill running. It looked like miles to the top. He labored up the rough path, fell in the darkness, tumbled back down a little way, pulled himself up, crying out the boy's name, "Alex, Alex," as he assailed the hill again. All the pain he felt he focused onto that creature's face, that creature he would destroy, and then he and the boy could find some peace. Yes, just over this hill, and then there would be the quarry, down into the quarry and the hut would be there, with the creature inside, expecting one of her victims, and he would destroy her.

"Was it jealousy?" Sean said. "Was it because they were legitimate? Was it — "

"If a loaded gun," the boy, cutting him off, explained,

"was put into my hand, I would point it at someone and pull its trigger. Because triggers are meant to be pulled, because a loaded gun is a fate. And then *everything* in your life changes. It's magical. I had a maths teacher once, Mr. Matthews. A more severe, immaculate, patrician man you could hardly imagine. Smelled of chalk and black tea, and sometimes very faintly of barley wine — an old man, bachelor all his life, who ate, drank, and breathed maths. Fearsome he was, and he used to lean over us and score up our sums with a vicious red pen. That's when you could smell him, see the broken veins in his cheeks, the wads of cotton wool he'd pushed into his ears for some reason. I was probably about eight or nine years old. And one day as he was leaning over me, massacring my work, I looked up at the side of his face, and it was as if that loaded gun had been placed into my hand. I leaned over and I kissed him — no one saw — right on the side of his mouth. He looked down at me — his old yellow eyes wide, his mouth trembling — as if I'd slipped a knife right into his heart." The boy paused and then emphatically repeated, "As if I'd slipped a knife *right into his heart*. And right there and then the world dissolved. Everything. After that, in the class, he became forgetful, sometimes would just stare abstractedly out of the window, seemed often nervous as if he'd never taught before; his clothes became slovenly. A month later we had a new maths teacher. We were told that Mr. Matthews had taken a leave of absence because of 'problems with his nerves.' Before the end of the year he was dead."

The word "dead" seemed to resonate in the air, the man and the boy staring at one another.

Finally Sean said, "So what was true? What in the diary was true?"

"I told you. It was all true. I just expressed it for her. That's what I'm here for. She had such a meager soul, but with the husbandry I've learned of necessity, I made quite a feast of it." The boy changed his tone suddenly into one of mock-fond remembrance. "You know what I used to love about Megan? When we screwed, her eyes used to roll and flutter. They went almost white, as if I were holding her by a thread of her hair over all the cold darkness between the stars. It was this she suckled on as I labored above her, as I watched her going blissfully blind and rooting at space, as only women can. And when I — "

"Shut your fucking mouth," Sean screamed, fragmented images of his daughter now scintillating in his head. Then Sean remembered the boy coming down to him to tell him that Liam wouldn't wake up, how beautifully acted the boy's anguish was, remembered finding his son, clean, pajamaed, and dead, as if death had passed like a breeze over him, like the scent of daffodils; and how the boy had stood beside him, pale and trembling, as they'd lowered Liam and then had lowered Megan into the ground; and imagined his wife's pain as she'd read the pages of that other diary. Not even memory was sacred. He'd even got into memory, had found his wife's wound and had pressed upon it mercilessly. Fake. Murderer. Soulless. Soulless.

"You're a liar." Violently, he thrust himself up to the

boy's face, spittle flying from his mouth as he shouted, "You're a liar. You're just an animal. You don't feel anything. You killed my life."

The boy widened his eyes, the left flickering, sticky with blood. He smiled and began to move his face toward Sean's, his mouth sensually open, his tongue playing lasciviously over his teeth. The man thrust him back with both hands, the boy's head making a thunderous crack as it struck the wall. The boy squeezed his eyes closed and then, grimly, came that smile that was beyond laughter in his face.

"And you know when she got pregnant," the boy said, his eyes still tight shut, that grim smile radiating a kind of abject triumph, "I managed to convince her that it was her own brother, reborn in her, that we were some kind of sacred triad and now had to enter the world of the dead. And she believed it, my poor, dear, dull Megan. God, how easy it is to get people to believe. In fact the only thing no one would believe is how little one has to offer for a soul. There's not even any thrill in it. It's like culling cattle, whole nations. You don't have to promise them eternity, you just have to lie with them in the darkness, and sometimes sing them a song. That's it!" The boy shouted this at the man as if the man were to blame, and the man responded by putting every ounce of his strength into striking the boy's face.

The boy hung his head slackly, blood and saliva coursing from his mouth.

Finally he looked back up at the man, speaking slowly, his face replete with grim triumph: "I'm your son, and you're nothing, nothing but a name on a piece of paper in a hole in the wall. You're nothing but a name."

"I never hurt your mother. I never hurt her," Sean said, his voice trembling.

"I was fathered and my mother was killed by every man who turns his head at a pair of legs."

And now suddenly the boy glanced away as if he'd seen something, sensed something out there in that forest of columns. For a moment he looked as if he were about to cry.

"Gordon," the boy shouted, "Gordon," as a bloody tear streamed from his left eye. "Oh, poor Caitlín," he whispered, turning back now to look at the man. "Why did she have to wander into this?"

"Into what?" Sean said, taking hold of the boy's shirt. "Who's Gordon? Where's Caitlín? Where is she?" He began to shake the boy, to bang his back against the wall. "Where is she?"

The boy just stared at him emptily, all triumph stripped from his abjectness, blood streaked all over his face. "Oh, Gordon," he whispered. "I hope you're on time."

The fatman crested the hill, and there, miles away, at the far side of the vast pit of the quarry, he saw the light of the cabin. He checked his watches, though hardly able to lift his arms. Some gave him time, just minutes, and some gave him none to cover those arduous miles, the scree winding down into the quarry. He felt spots of light around his heart, a terrible stitch in his side, like a hole out of which his breath was being leeched. He wasn't going to make it. For his own life. But he pushed on, because if he stopped there was nothing. And time was not yet up, one minute, three minutes, hurling himself on. Those spots of light, as he descended, stumbling, into the quarry, now flickered open, pierced him, so many slender blades, light cutting through clouds, cutting the breath right out of his neck. He felt a surge like a sudden wash of blood at the back of his head. The darkness had taken him by the throat with its bright teeth.

Wide bovine eyes incredulous, dumbly incredulous, he sank to the ground.

19:59. Caitlín, deeply relieved, got up from the bed to go. Then, as she looked at the door, a cold finger seemed to run down her spine. She shuddered and felt a foreboding about what was lying behind the door, about leaving this cell of light for the darkness of the quarry. She felt the boy somewhere out there in the darkness, felt him ever behind her, his face manifesting itself at these small dirty windows. Yes, if she just stared at them long enough, his face would appear from the darkness, lovely, alluring, and malign. Fear, like her childhood fear of dark mirrors and dark windows. Still it was not eight. Still the boy had a few seconds, but now she felt that he would not come in, *could not* enter from the darkness, and that when she opened the door, the darkness would be standing before her, smiling like an evil enigma, a smile beyond laughter. And now, behind her, as she placed her hand on the handle of the door, she heard the hum of that cassette-clock-radio as the 19:59 rotated into 20:00. Girding herself, she turned the handle of the door just as the numbers clicked into place.

"Caitlín."

Behind her. It was the boy. Spinning around, almost collapsing with shock, she fell back against the door. Silence. Her stomach felt as if it had turned to liquid, and then his voice came again, a voice that was breaking, the child struggling against the man in him. But the song itself was oblivious to the struggle, far beyond it, medieval, lilting and yet viscous, sweet and heavy with the pain of things forgotten, gone.

> I dreamed I were so great for her.
> That I was only me she dreamed.
> I dreamed for her I lived forever.
> She dreamed me dead to deepen love.
> So I dreamed myself a monument,
> And dead indeed with silent face,
> So she might suffer constantly —
> But Constant was she not to me,
> And another loves she now.

With a click, the tape in the cassette-clock-radio switched off.

Caitlín gathered herself, the shock still congealing in her veins as she left the hut and ran, as in a nightmare, through the dark quarry and up to her car.

The ashen desolation of his fury. Now Caitlín too. That was everyone. Almost everyone. He couldn't seem to see the boy's face. It swarmed with features, became women and men, boys and girls, wanton and chaste, lovely and grotesque. He couldn't stop it from swarming. Lifting the iron bar high above his head, he looked into the face of a monster. But just as, with all his strength, he swung the bar down, just as it was too late to stop, that face suddenly stilled. The boy had closed his eyes, gently, like a child calmed from a nightmare, a child no longer fearful of sleep.